MATED to the CAPO

Portal City Protectors Book 1

GEORGETTE ST. CLAIR

Text copyright © 2019 Georgette St. Clair

All Rights Reserved in accordance with the U.S. Copyright Act of 1976, the scanning, uploading, and electronic sharing of any part of this book without the permission of the publisher or author constitute unlawful piracy and theft of the author's intellectual property. If you would like to use material from this book (other than for review purposes), prior written permission must be obtained by contacting the publisher at info@beyonddeflit.com. Thank you for your support of authors' rights.

FBI Anti-Piracy Warning: The unauthorized reproduction or distribution of a copyrighted work is illegal. Criminal copyright infringement, including infringement without monetary gain, is investigated by the FBI and is punishable by up to five years in federal prison along with a fine of $250,000.

This book is a work of fiction. Any references to historical events, real people, or real places are used fictitiously. Other names, characters, places, and events are products of the author's imagination, and any resemblance to actual events or places or persons living or dead is entirely coincidental.

Beyond DEF

https://www.beyonddeflit.com

Editing – Tiffany Fox and C.A. Houghton; Beyond DEF
Cover design – LeTeisha Newton; Beyond DEF
Interior Layout: Deena Rae Schoenfeldt; E-Book Builders for Beyond DEF

BOOKS BY GEORGETTE

Portal City Protectors
Mated to the Capo
Mated to the Enforcer
Mated to the Prince

The Alpha Billion-weres
The Billion-were Needs a Mate
A Cub for the Billion-were
The Billion-were Claims His Mate

Timber Valley Pack
Bride of the Alpha
Purr for the Alpha
Hard as Steele
Lynx on the Loose
Taken by the Alpha
Won't Be Denied

Shifters, Inc.
The Alpha Meets His Match
His Purrfect Mate
Pixie the Lion Tamer
The Bear Who Loved Me
Spotting His Leopard
Blackmailed by the Wolf

Blue Moon Junction
The Alpha Claims a Mate
The Bobcat's Tale
Hard to Bear
My Heart Laid Bear

Starcrossed Dating Agency
The Vulfan's True Mate
The Dragon Claims His Treasure
The Vulfan's Dark Desires

The Mating Game
Big Bad Wolf
Dating a Dragon
A Grizzly Kind of Love

Alpha Prime
Shiftily Ever After
His Curvy Mate

Bridenapped
The Alpha Chronicles
The Alpha's Choice

Shifters of Silver Peak
Mate Marked
Mate for a Month
A Very Shifty Christmas

Tri-Valley Dragon
Bride of the Dragon
Love Burns

Twin Alphas
Claimed
Desired

Neck Deep
Neck Deep in Trouble
Neck Deep in Vampires

Curvy Girls
The Big Girl and the Bounty Hunter
Sweet Surrender
Claimed by the Cowboy

Standalones
I Married a Warlock
Like Cats and Dogs
Lion's Den
The Dragon's Christmas Wish
Shifter's Solace
Furrever Yours

MATED TO THE *CAPO*

After an epically bad blind date, Zoey Monroe swore off men forever and got a tattoo that says "love bites." Maybe she shouldn't have tempted fate. A very powerful Mafia wolf has bitten her on the ass on a full moon. According to the Moretti Pack, the "moon-bite" means she is now the mate of Dominic Lombardi.

Dominic will follow Zoey to the ends of the earth—no matter how far she runs or how well she hides. Crowding her world and refusing to take no for an answer, he refuses to stop courting her until she becomes his wife.

New dangers suddenly rear their ugly heads and threaten all of Encantado, the supernatural sin city Zoey calls home. When dark magic arrives, will she stop running long enough for her werewolf to claim his bride, or will she find herself fitted with a cement overcoat and sleeping with the fishes?

MATED to the CAPO

CHAPTER ONE

Zoey limped through the door of Kalinda's Katering Saturday morning wondering if she'd be picking up her paycheck or facing a firing squad.

After the week she'd had, the firing squad would be par for the course.

Her favorite cafe had closed up shop and vanished last Monday—the latest in a string of local businesses that had shut down.

Then, an acquaintance had set up a blind date four nights ago, describing the guy as "perfect for you." She must not have liked Zoey very much because Mr. "Perfect for you" had become the blind date from hell. Five minutes after meeting her, the drunken accountant had slurred that he "liked dating fat chicks because they weren't so demanding." Well, that was a guaranteed panty-dropper … not.

When Zoey had made it clear she was going home alone, he stiffed her with the check, so she'd headed to the bar. As far as she could recall, she'd tried to drink her weight in tequila, which was why she'd found the phrase "love bites" tattooed on her right butt cheek the next morning. The fact the calligraphy was really pretty didn't help anything.

Last night proved those sucktastic events had been the high points of her week.

Zoey entered Kalinda's office, trying to keep her limp to a minimum. Clad in her usual uniform of tuxedo jacket and skirt, her dark shiny hair yanked back in a severe braid and brows drawn together, Kalinda stood. She was tall, mocha-skinned, and regal. Judging by the curt look she fixed on Zoey, she was also very annoyed. Quite the opposite, Zoey was short, plump, and her brown hair exploded everywhere in unruly waves.

The expression on Kalinda's face told Zoey her boss had already heard what had happened at the Moretti Pack's party. Of course. Word got around fast in Encantado.

"Hello, Kalinda. Beautiful morning, isn't it? The sun is shining, the phoenixes are flocking …" She gestured out the window at the half-dozen phoenixes gliding overhead, trailing cold blue flames.

The business district was typical, gaudy Encantado, with a kind of tarted-up chorus girl appeal to it. Architectural styles mish-mashed together, emphasizing a mid-century modern feel, and spindly, fifty-foot palm trees lined the streets. Neon signs were splashed randomly up and down the avenue. Kalinda's Katering was located in a strip of three-story office buildings, squeezed in between a wholesaler dealing in ingredients for spells and a company which specialized in tours through "Encantado's Most Magical Neighborhoods." One of their buses, painted like a dragon and full of excited tourists, was gliding out of the parking lot.

But today, Kalinda was in no mood to admire the scenery.

"There are three simple rules to catering a mafia pack event," Kalinda said, her voice sharp enough to slice through bone.

"You don't say. Why don't you tell them to me." Zoey might have been a little salty, but she felt she had the right. Her right butt cheek had an enormous set of fang marks in it, right below the tattoo, and the bite was probably going to scar.

"Get in. Don't get bitten. Get out. Is that so hard to remember?"

Zoey shrugged. "Apparently."

Like Zoey hadn't heard this lecture before. After all, Zoey worked those events all the time. She was one of the few girls willing to work the Moretti Pack shindigs because everyone else was terrified of them.

Zoey was too, of course. Shifters were scary enough, but the Moretti Pack? Effing petrifying. They'd been known to literally eat their enemies. The pay was too good to resist though. It paid triple what she earned at other catering gigs.

Kalinda gave her a dirty look. "Now is not the time for your sass."

"When *is* the time?" she grumbled. Could she schedule a time? But she didn't say it out loud because Kalinda looked like she was about to blow a gasket.

"When you didn't do something to provoke a *Capo* of the Moretti Pack to bite you on the ass."

Zoey looked at Kalinda, eyes widening in alarm. "How do you know he's a *Capo*? I didn't know he was a *Capo*."

"Word gets around fast. What did you do to him? Step on his paw? Pull his tail?"

"Do you think I'm crazy?" Zoey spluttered. "Seriously? You think I'd pull the tail of any wolf shifter, much less a Made Wolf?"

There were made wolves, and there were Made Wolves. Dominic Lombardi was both.

The tattoo on the back of Dominic's hand told a story. The howling wolf nestled into a crescent moon meant he was a Made Wolf—he'd had to prove his loyalty to the pack by secret, violent means. The star above it meant he hadn't been born a wolf.

From what Zoey had heard, surviving the Turn took exceptional strength and stamina.

Dominic ignored Zoey, other than grunting a curt "thank you" when she served him drinks. If anything, he was even more abrupt with Zoey than he was with the other servers, although he didn't flirt with them or anything.

But Zoey hadn't known he was a *Capo*. That meant he was one of very few men who served directly under Arturo Moretti, the *Capo di tutti Capi*—boss of all bosses. Arturo tore people's limbs off for just looking at him wrong.

Zoey paced in front of Kalinda's desk, her butt cheek aching with each step. *Stupid bite!* It figured that the only time Dominic's mouth was near her nether regions, he was in wolf form, sinking his fangs into her flesh.

She mentally slapped herself for that thought. Dominic was nothing but a very naughty fantasy—a fantasy involving blue-green eyes that would make the ocean jealous, a perfect butt, and muscular thighs. Even if she could have him, she wouldn't because of who he worked for.

"The no-shift potion is guaranteed, right?" Zoey raised a brow.

"Of course," Kalinda said, sliding her gaze away from her friend. "I'm pretty sure."

Zoey spun around and pinned her with a glare of fury. "*Pretty sure?!*" she screeched.

Kalinda threw up her hands in frustration. "Warlock Cyrus is the best in the district. I have never heard a complaint against him. The only way we can be sure, though, is if someone was bitten and went through the next full moon without turning. None of my girls have ever been bitten. The potion is strictly a precaution. A couple of times, the Moretti men got a little frisky when they were in wolf form and maybe, ah, nipped a girl. Or two."

"Or two? So … like five or six?" Zoey glowered at her boss.

Kalinda's gaze moved to the left. "Three or four. Through their clothing. They didn't even draw blood, but I didn't want to take any chances, so I started using the no-shift. I have never, ever heard of it failing, so we're good there." Kalinda's lips twitched up in what was probably supposed to be a reassuring smile, but it looked so forced, it had the opposite effect. And it was out of place on her face.

Kalinda was a worrier, a caretaker, a fixer, an organizer. But not a smiler.

"You never mentioned the nipping when you hired me," Zoey said indignantly.

Kalinda looked her up and down with a critical eye, ignoring her complaint. "Do you suddenly crave raw meat? Are you unusually hairy?"

Zoey gingerly sank down into a chair, favoring her right butt cheek, and gave Kalinda look of annoyance. "I was bitten at two a.m. Seven hours ago. It's probably too soon to tell. The next full moon isn't for twenty-eight days. And the werewolves don't have any craving for raw meat when they're in human form. You know that. Do they order a hundred pounds of hamburger? No, the pack gets filet mignon and prime rib."

"Right, right." Kalinda sat in the chair next to Zoey's and nervously tapped her fingers on the chair arm, her long, gold-painted nails clicking on the scarred wood. "Pardon my panicking. This only involves one of my employees possibly accidentally offending a pack of wolf-men who delight in eviscerating their enemies. Why would I be a little tense? Okay, walk me through what happened. Tell me everything that led up to him biting you."

Zoey leaned back in the chair and closed her eyes. "Let me think a minute." She tried to stifle an enormous yawn. She hadn't slept all night. The room she rented above a nightclub had paper-thin walls. Not to mention it was hard to sleep after having been bitten in the butt by a werewolf.

"Fine, fine, I'll get you some coffee," Kalinda said grudgingly. She liked to act like a hardass—to run any kind of business in Encantado, she had to—but she was protective of the girls who worked for her.

Zoey nodded gratefully. "You're a lifesaver."

As Kalinda hurried off to the kitchen in the back, Zoey replayed yesterday through her mind, searching for clues.

Why had Dominic chomped on her gluteus? Was it because she'd asked to talk to his boss? It hadn't seemed like a terrible idea at the time.

The Moretti Pack was supposed to ensure city services made their way in and out of all the districts in their territory. They certainly charged the districts enough for their "protection". They'd been taking money from District 17 for months now and hadn't delivered a damn thing.

Yesterday, she'd reached her boiling point. As the trash pickup had become more and more sporadic over the last few months, rats crawled around the piles of garbage rotting in the streets. She had stepped in the runoff and ruined her new sneakers. And the potholes? Forget about it. She worked as a bike messenger during the week, and riding through her neighborhood was like running a slalom course.

It had gotten to the point where Zoey and the other residents were paying their extortion money just for the privilege of not being murdered by a pack of corrupt, furry goombahs. Yes, they didn't pay as much as the wealthy districts, which meant they could only expect the bare minimum of services, but now they weren't even getting that.

When the neighborhood residents tried to take the trash to the city dump themselves, they were charged an outrageous fee.

Zoey was part of a volunteer neighborhood improvement committee. She and the other committee members had tried to talk to Jordan Smythe, the pack's neighborhood liaison who collected their fees and passed them on to the Moretti Pack. The results? Crickets.

And more garbage.

Zoey's tired mind was drifting. She mentally gave herself a shake and replayed the events of the previous night.

It had been a gorgeous evening. The pack threw a party to celebrate thirty years of Arturo's leadership. Enormous potted palms and winding stone paths surrounded the exotically landscaped garden. A fat white moon hung lazily in a velvet sky, and a warm breeze swept the scent of magnolia blossoms through the air.

Arturo was sitting by himself when Zoey tried to approach him. His men were scattered around drinking expensive whiskey, smoking cigars, and helping themselves to the lavish buffet. The *Capo di tutti Capi* looked as if he was actually in a good mood. Lounging in a wicker chair and sipping a glass of Pappy Van Winkle, he stared off into the distance at the twinkling lights of the city's skyscrapers and a single pegasus flying overhead.

Zoey had walked over to Ottavio, one of Arturo's men, and asked if she could be granted an audience to address an issue in District 17. She had been told that was the proper way to approach Arturo – through one of his men, and only after asking in a very deferential tone.

Ottavio nodded gravely and stood, towering over her, but before he could answer, Dominic bit her.

She didn't see how the two could be related. She really didn't think she had offended anyone. She had spoken with the utmost respect, and Ottavio hadn't looked angry. And she'd been speaking to him, not Dominic. If Dominic had been angry at her, he wouldn't have just nipped her. He'd have torn her in half.

Kalinda hurried back in, shoving a cracked mug of coffee into Zoey's hands, and then leaned on her desk. "It's instant. We save the good stuff for the customers," Kalinda said.

Zoey took a long swig of it and made a face. "Yeah, you do."

"So talk. How did you bring the wrath of the wolf down on you? What have you done, Zoey?"

"Nothing," she said, with a wide-eyed, innocent expression, and took another sip, grimacing at the bitterness.

In hindsight, maybe she shouldn't have tried to speak to Arturo at all. Whatever the problem was, he had to know about it already, right?

"Okay, you wanted a recap," she said quickly. "I showed up at the event, and nothing seemed out of the ordinary. Dominic was in human form. He did glance my way once, but most of the night, he talked with a few people and pretty much ignored me. One of them was a tall, good-looking guy with a scarred face. I think his name's Romano, and he's always with Dominic at all the parties. I think he's an enforcer. One of them was Giuliana, she's Arturo's personal assistant and niece, and one was a dark-haired girl who kept following Dominic around and petting his arm." She tried to keep the snarkiness out of her voice when she mentioned the dark-haired girl—she'd mostly succeeded.

Dominic had acted like he was casual friends with the blonde and looked bored with the dark-haired girl, which had made Zoey happier than it should have.

Kalinda frowned. "Dark-haired girl. Hmm. For some reason that makes me nervous."

"Everything makes you nervous," Zoey pointed out.

Kalinda made a skeptical "psssht" noise and glanced out the window. A day-walker in a black cape strolled by. Day-walkers were rich-as-hell vampires who'd paid good money for powerful charms that made them temporarily immune to sunlight. The wards affixed to the window glowed as he walked by. It cost Kalinda a small dragon's hoard to keep those wards charged. Kalinda's wards were a lot stronger than those on Zoey's apartment building.

A lion shifter in human form walked by. At least, she was pretty sure it was a lion shifter—they all had thick, tawny-blond hair that flowed past their shoulders. The shifter accidentally jostled the vampire, and the vampire swung to face him with a snarl. A long, tense moment stretched between them before they finally went their separate ways.

"Of course, everything makes me nervous," Kalinda said irritably. "Anyone who lives in Encantado and isn't nervous has their head up their ass."

Zoey shrugged. Yes, living in a Portal City was fairly terrifying on a regular basis, given that the portals tended to burp out scary, hostile creatures at random. They never knew if the mages would be able to hold them off, but she just didn't see the point in being afraid all the time.

"I dunno," she said. "What good does it do to worry? If I'm fated to be hexed or dragon roasted, I might as well enjoy my life up until the last moment. And try to make sure that everyone around me is too. If I'm not fated for a terrible death, then I'd have spent a lot of time worrying about nothing."

"Fine, Saccharine Sally, nothing scares you. Just keep in mind, fearlessness isn't going to make you any less tasty next time we have a troll attack. Now, finish telling me what happened." Kalinda fixed Zoey with her fierce glare.

Zoey nodded, trying to remember. "Well, he ignored me the rest of the night. After the moon rose, they all started getting louder and friskier and a couple of older guys pinched my butt, and I *accidentally* spilled a drink on one of them and stepped on the other one's foot." Kalinda had told her to do that. Those kinds of macho guys would run right over the girls if they didn't stand up for themselves.

"And then?"

She hesitated. Kalinda wouldn't be too happy if she found out Zoey had tried to approach the boss of the Moretti Pack with a complaint at one of Kalinda's events. She'd probably slap Zoey silly or fire her on the spot.

"Well, I was standing there with a tray of hors d'oeuvres when I felt a sharp pain in my butt. My right cheek, in case that matters." That wasn't strictly a lie. She had indeed been standing there holding a tray.

"It doesn't," Kalinda assured her with a scowl of impatience.

"I dropped the tray and screamed. When I spun around, there was this huge, beautiful white wolf staring at me intensely. I recognized it as Dominic because he had the same blue-green eyes and ... and I don't know, I could just tell it was him. I was so shocked, I dropped my tray and ran." She finished the rest of the coffee and set the cup on a small side table. "So ... that shifting potion ..."

"I already told you. I've never heard of it failing."

Well, that wasn't super reassuring. From what she'd heard, being bitten by a warrior-class shifter would be a guaranteed ticket to the nearest mortuary if the potion didn't work. To survive their bite, a person had to have a large physique and the constitution of a world-class athlete.

At this point, though, all she could do was wait twenty-eight days and hope not to die at the next full moon. Fun!

Kalinda opened her mouth to ask her something else when she looked out her window and sucked in her breath.

"Go to the kitchen," Kalinda said in a low, urgent tone. "Now."

CHAPTER Two

Zoey followed Kalinda's gaze, and her heart stuttered in her chest. Dominic, Romano, and Giuliana were climbing out of a van that had just pulled up to the curb in front of Kalinda's building. She shot out of the office, closing the door behind her.

Kalinda's legendary kitchen of deliciousness was fortunately close enough to the office that Zoey could eavesdrop. The air was rich with the aroma of a thousand ingredients, which should help disguise her scent in case the wolves tried to sniff her out.

She closed the door, her stomach churning with worry. If anything happened, she had no power to defend herself. Like the vast majority of magic-bloods, her magic was just strong enough to be detectible by the authorities—and it was utterly useless. She had earth magic; her houseplants were super healthy, and she could make flowers bloom faster. Give her a handful of buds and she could make them burst into blossom if she concentrated hard enough. Woo hoo!

It had completely upended her life. She'd been living in San Francisco when her magic talent was discovered during a random sweep by the Federal Bureau of Magical Containment. Thanks to FBMC, she'd been ripped away from her home and her job at an internet startup and had been given her choice of portal cities. She'd picked Encantado because Nevada was reasonably near her family who lived in Marin County.

She also had map magic—she could find her way anywhere. It was a form of earth magic, the same as her green thumb. She was like a human GPS, but with electronic GPS available, her power was more useless than a screen door on a submarine. She'd have given up her powers in a heartbeat if she could.

Unfortunately, it wasn't an option, and neither was leaving Encantado. Ever.

Magic-bloods weren't allowed to live outside of the Enchanted Zones. Non-magics tended to get very nervous about magical folk living among them. They were afraid the magic-bloods would cast spells on them or bite them.

That was only sometimes true.

And from what Zoey had heard, most of the other portal cities weren't any safer. The Pendulum Swing of the 1950s had caused all this mess. Magic had torn through the areas where the veil between universes was thin. The cities and towns in the affected zones were rife with danger. High-level mages, vampires, and shifters battled for power, and the low-level mages and human population—approximately seventy-five percent—were frequently caught in the crossfire.

But right now, Zoey had more pressing concerns than her reluctant relocation to Encantado.

Like, had Dominic decided she was irresistibly tasty and come to finish what he'd started?

The front door banged open, and the thud of footsteps filled the silence.

"We're looking for a waitress named Zoey Monroe," Dominic announced, his voice loud and booming.

"Ah, yes, I heard something about one of your men biting her," Kalinda said. "I'm sorry, she isn't here. It was very distressing to hear of her being bitten. Were you displeased with her services?" She kept her voice respectful but firm.

"My wolf bit her, and I was not displeased. We call it a moon-bite, or a moon-claim."

Say what now? Zoey's knees wobbled.

"Excuse me?" Kalinda's voice rose to a pitch Zoey had never heard before.

"My wolf has chosen her as a mate."

"That doesn't make sense. If she's your mate, why wouldn't your wolf have bitten her before?"

"Are you hard of hearing?" Dominic snapped. "I spoke clearly enough. Full moon. My wolf never encountered her on a full moon before."

"But … she's not a shifter!" Kalinda protested.

"It doesn't matter. She can bear my pups as long as she's a magic-blood, and I smelled the magic in her."

Ewww. Rude.

Zoey lifted her arm and surreptitiously sniffed. Her lilac deodorant was still working. What exactly did magic smell like? Did it smell bad?

"Why her?" Kalinda demanded. "There are plenty of other girls who are more …"

"More what?" Dominic snapped with a hint of danger in his voice.

Yes, more what? Zoey wanted to know too. More attractive? That seemed to be the only possible answer, and it stung. Yes, she was a little on the full-figured side. Her mother always said that just meant there was more of her to love. As for her freckles, her mother used to call them angel kisses.

"More, ah, willing!" Kalinda said brightly. "She's the independent type. I happen to know for a fact she's not looking for a relationship right now."

"Too bad. That will change." Dominic's voice turned rough and impatient. "My wolf chose Zoey, and Zoey I will have. Now, you know I can scent her. And the scent is fresh. You can bring her out here, or I can tear the place apart."

"Go ahead and look around," Kalinda offered loudly. "She stopped by here to pick up her pay and left a few minutes ago. That's why you're scenting her."

Kalinda clearly meant for her to overhear that.

Zoey opened the door to the alley. One way led to the parking lot in front of Kalinda's office—bad idea because the shifters had parked there—and the other led to another alleyway between two rows of buildings.

She dashed toward the other alleyway and raced around the corner.

His mate? Is he serious?

She had to find some way to convince him he didn't really want to claim her. Heck, given her past dating history, that shouldn't be too hard. Apparently, one night out with her was enough to do it for most guys.

Zoey stopped and stood still, picturing her apartment, her magic searching for the clearest, safest path.

Her map magic not only guided her to any destination she could visualize in her head, it also sensed obstacles between her and her destination.

Of course, knowing obstacles were there didn't help much if she was surrounded.

Her magic froze up, twisting in indecision, as a man leaped over a six-foot chain-link fence in a single bound, clearing it easily and landing with a resounding thud a few feet in front of her.

Dominic—the man who'd chomped her cheek the night before and now thought he was her *husband*. Mate. Whatever. He was sexy as hell, yeah, but she barely knew the guy. He was also the *Capo* of one of the most violent and corrupt mafia shifter packs on the entire West Coast. She kind of had issues with how his pack ran things.

He didn't seem to care what she thought about the whole claiming thing. He looked down at her, his mouth curled in cruel amusement and his blue eyes glinting. "Hello … mate."

Her foolish heart fluttered in her chest, and her lady-bits dampened.

Dominic was a criminal, from a pack of criminals. They were killers. Arsonists. Extortionists. She'd seen the burned-out shells of businesses that had refused to pay protection. She'd watched the police haul away the bodies of their victims and toss them into the middle of the street to deliver a message: anyone who crossed them would come to a swift, brutal end.

Hell, she was paying their lousy protection money and not getting a thing in return. They weren't even honest thugs.

Yet she couldn't stop staring. So much pretty.

She cleared her throat. "Hello, person who bit me on the ass last night. It still hurts, by the way." She folded her arms across her chest and gave him her best intimidating scowl. That was hard to do when she had to tip her head back because he stood a good foot taller than her.

He just stood there smirking as Romano and Giuliana came trotting down the alley. Giuliana, delicate looking and deceptively elegant in her designer jeans and spike-heeled pumps, looked her up and down with narrow-eyed suspicion. Romano, tall and burly and handsome despite severe scarring on one side of his face, just looked amused.

Dominic flicked a glance at them, and then his gaze settled on Zoe again, his eyes glowing with that strange shifter light. Zoe fought not to drop her gaze because then her eyes would drift to the area below his belt, which had an alarmingly large bulge. She knew because she'd sneaked a peek or two when delivering his drinks.

"Hello, Zoey. You're looking positively delicious. By the way, you were in the kitchen hiding from us, which means that your boss is a liar. How shall I kill her?"

Well, that was a bucket of ice water dumped right on her libido. "Excuse me. That's your idea of flirting with me?" she spluttered with fury.

He cocked his head to one side. "I don't have to flirt with you. You're my mate. Well, you will be at the next full moon."

"Well, either that or I'll be dead." She shrugged with forced casualness. "Or shifted, but from what I've heard, most people don't survive a bite from the warrior class."

"*You* might." Giuliana's lip curled slightly. Only physically large humans had the slightest chance of surviving the change.

"Oh, was that a size joke? So very original," Zoey fake-clapped. "Unfortunately, you'll have to try harder. That barely ranked a one on the 'ouch, my poor feelings' scale."

Dominic pinned the petite blonde with an ice-cold glare. "Giuliana. Apologize."

"Sorry." Giuliana lifted one skinny shoulder in a shrug. Her tone was conciliatory but her expression was not.

Dominic returned his attention to Zoey. "The potion Kalinda uses has never failed. You will survive to be my mate."

Zoey took a step back, and he took a step forward. She held up her hands in a "stop" motion. "Whoa there! You're entering my personal space bubble. Now, let's start with Kalinda. If you kill her, I will hate you forever and either murder you in your sleep or die trying." His lips curled in an amused grin. "Okay, let's be realistic, definitely the latter. But Kalinda was trying to protect me. You protect your pack-mates, don't you?"

"You're human, so she's not your pack." Dominic shrugged. "But point taken. I will grant her an exemption this one time." He glanced at one of his pack-mates. "Romano, don't kill the tasty morsel."

Romano let out a disappointed groan. "But she smelled so good, and I haven't had lunch."

"You and your stomach!" Dominic said, exasperated. "Go grab a sandwich. I need to talk to my mate."

Giuliana scowled. "We're letting her get away with lying to us? This sets a bad precedent for the pack."

"Last I checked, I outrank you," Dominic said with a hint of a snarl in his voice. "Unless you're going to try to play the 'my uncle is the *Capo di tutti Capi*' card."

"You can kiss my ass!" Giuliana spat, her face flushing red with anger.

"I could, but now I have a mate. So actually, I can't. Romano's still single, though, unless something's changed since last night."

"Still on the market. And quite a catch," Romano leered at Giuliana.

Giuliana saluted Dominic and Romano with both middle fingers and stormed off. Romano jogged after her—thankfully, in the opposite direction from Kalinda's office.

"You were seriously going to kill my boss?" Zoey was appalled. That was a new low. Killing rival pack members was bad enough, but murdering a woman for trying to protect her employee and friend?

"I guess we'll never know." He took another step forward, so Zoey took a step back, but his stride was longer than hers, so he was gaining on her.

"You don't actually want to be mated to me," she argued.

He cocked his head to the side. "Now, what makes you think that? I came for you, didn't I?"

"You … well …" she gestured at her soft, curvy body, "you're handsome as sin and you're a Moretti Capo. You could have anyone."

"Thank you!" Dominic beamed at her and gave a deep, theatrical bow. "I'm glad you agree. And since you qualify as 'anyone', that means I can have you. You can stop inching backward now. Yes, I noticed."

She stopped moving. Damned predator vision. "I meant you could have someone more suitable! More … uh … skinnier!"

"More skinnier?" His eyes gleamed with fierce mockery. "Bad grammar? Now that's just beneath you."

She tried to make him burst into flames with the power of her glare and failed. Damn her useless magic. She knew a witch who could raise blisters. That would come in handy right about now.

"You know what I meant."

"Not really. Why would I want less woman when I could have more?"

That temporarily threw her for a loop. Why, indeed? Zoey actually liked that answer. No, she loved it. She couldn't find a single thing wrong with it.

She refused to give in just because he suddenly was being charming and funny. He was a vicious murdering criminal. A hot, sexy, but vicious, but charismatic … Wait, where was she going with this?

"We don't even know each other!"

"My wolf selected you. He has impeccable taste." His eyes glowed briefly as he mentioned his wolf. That eye glow thing happened a lot with shifters, especially when they got excited. It never failed to freak her the hell out.

"That doesn't make sense. I know your pack has arranged matings. I catered a wedding for one. Their mating had been arranged since birth, in fact."

"True," he acknowledged. "Arturo has been searching for an appropriate mate for me for some time now. Giuliana was a possibility, but then the Bianchi Pack approached us about arranging a mating with Fabiana, the dark-haired woman at the party last night."

For some reason, that statement made her feel prickly all over, as if she'd rolled in a nettle bush.

Dominic shrugged. "My wolf never really took to either one of them, but for the good of the pack, I would have paired with whomever Arturo decreed." He grinned fiercely at her. "But then you came along and my wolf had other ideas. How lucky for me."

"No wonder Giuliana doesn't like me."

"Oh, she's not jealous. She didn't want the mating. She would have obeyed her uncle because nobody says no to Arturo, but when Arturo revealed he was considering Fabiana, she said, and I quote, 'Thank fuck.'" He smirked, seemingly amused.

She frowned. "But … what if you went through the arranged mating and then met me on a full moon?"

"You want to know how things work with shifters?" He snorted. "We don't reveal all of our secrets to outsiders. Come home with me, and I'll be happy to enlighten you."

"Home, with you?" She couldn't believe he was even bothering to ask, rather than just kidnapping her. "I'd rather French-kiss a bridge troll that hadn't gargled in a month."

"Since they gargle with human blood, that's probably wise."

He took another step toward her. She tried to jump back, but he lunged forward and grabbed her by the arm. The touch of his hand sent a shock through her body.

"Here's what's going to happen. I am going to court you. You are going to give me a really hard time, which is just going to make the chase that much more fun. And then you're going to give in and we'll have amazingly hot sex. You'll be mine on the next full moon, and some day you'll be asking yourself why you ever thought it would be a good idea to try to run from a Moretti wolf."

Zoey's heart hammered in her chest, and she swallowed hard. He smelled of musk and some kind of delicious spicy cologne, and his nearness was scrambling her senses.

She cleared her throat. "I'm sorry, I don't speak lunatic, so I zoned out for a few seconds. Are we finished? I've got things to do. Wolves to hide from."

He smiled at her kindly, as if talking to someone who was very simple. "Here's a question for you. Why are you fighting this? You're very attracted to me. I can scent it on you."

"Eww! Stop saying you can smell things on me!" she protested, jerking at her arm. He tightened his fingers until she stopped resisting. She kicked him in the shin, which made him laugh. Damned mafia cave-wolf ass-face.

"I'm a wolf, sweetheart, get used to it. It's not as if it's unpleasant. Do you hear me complaining? It's delightful, actually. And it's getting stronger. You like to wrestle, don't you?" His grin was the sexiest thing she'd ever seen. It wrapped around her and melted her defenses, stroking secret parts of her deep inside. Why did evil have to be so attractive? "We like that too. Our men are pretty rough with our women, but in a good way. I promise, you won't hear any complaints."

Her cheeks flamed hot with embarrassment, and she wished the cracks in the sidewalk would open up to swallow her.

"I'm not your sweetheart."

Dominic maneuvered her toward the alley wall. She stumbled as he backed her up, and he steadied her easily.

"Darling, then? Babe?" His smirk stretched wider.

"You want to know why I'm resisting? Because you're a member of the Moretti Pack, and …"

His eyes darkened from the color of a summer sky to the color of a stormy sea.

"Watch yourself," he growled, and Zoey felt an icy shiver of fear. His loyalty to his pack and his boss would be absolute.

"I wouldn't fit in with that lifestyle," she said carefully. *Because you're a corrupt, thieving, murdering, blackmailing bunch of assholes.* "I'm a goody two shoes. I'm the law-and-order type. I return my library books on time, and I wait for the light to change before I cross."

He looked at her skeptically. "Not from Encantado, are you?"

So he hadn't had time to find out much about her.

"No, so I'm completely unsuitable."

"Nice try. I like how you keep trying to fight this. Do you know what happens when prey runs from a predator?"

Zoey stared up at him, trying to speak, but the words dried up in her throat.

When prey runs from a predator, the predator gives chase.

Suddenly, Dominic leaned in and kissed her. She definitely was going to slap the hell out of him for taking liberties, but she somehow forgot to fight back.

His lips were soft as pillows, and her lips parted in surprise. He tasted like mint as his tongue probed her mouth, swirling gently in an intimate dance. He cradled the back of her head gently as the kiss went on and on, and she melted like taffy under his heat.

Zoey sank into a daze of sensation, the world falling away. She was no longer in a gritty alley next to an overflowing dumpster. She was on a plane where only she and Dominic existed. Traffic sounds faded, and the beat of her heart thudded in her ears.

And then he let go and stepped away.

She stood there, astonished.

That's it? He wasn't going to throw her over his shoulder and haul her off to his wolf-cave or wherever he lived?

Dominic winked at her, turned, and walked off. Zoey stared after him, reluctantly admiring the view and wondering why she didn't feel more relieved. He'd let her go. Her map-sense told her the obstacles between here and home had vanished, leaving a clear path.

Did "mate" mean something entirely different than she thought?

Whatever. She waited a couple of minutes to be sure he was gone before retrieving her bicycle from where it was chained up in front of Kalinda's office. She raced through the streets as if the hounds of hell were on her heels. Her butt still throbbed with every push of the pedals. When would it stop?

As she pulled up in front of her building, the stink of sun-heated trash flooded her nostrils, and rats scampered across the street, unafraid. She was almost tempted to say yes to Dominic's ... er, proposal? Demands? Maybe then she could ask him to have the Moretti Pack do their damned job. But no, she wasn't going to make a lifelong commitment just to get someone to take out the trash.

She was pretty sure her future husband-slash-mate had just abandoned her anyway. He came on all strong, kissed her stupid, and then walked away. Maybe he didn't like the way she kissed, which kind of stung, but it also meant she was free. So ... that was good news, right?

But he'd mentioned something about her being his mate twenty-eight days from now. Was he going to try to claim her, or was he giving up on the whole idea completely? Nothing made sense.

Zoey was afraid to go to her apartment, in case there was a Moretti squad waiting to ambush her. But after a night without sleep, she was wiped out. If she didn't take a nap soon, she'd fall asleep on her feet. When she got home, she sank down onto her couch, bleary with exhaustion, and fell asleep with the memory of Dominic's lips on hers.

CHAPTER THREE

While eating lunch, Dominic received a text from Arturo summoning him to the Arena, an entertainment resort with casinos, magic shows, and no-holds-barred cage fighting. It was also owned by the Moretti Pack.

He and Romano left their steaks half-eaten and made the forty-minute, cross-town drive in fifteen minutes, leaving behind a trail of near-accidents and furiously honking horns. It didn't matter. When Arturo called, his wolves hauled ass.

The Arena was easy to find. Anyone just needed to look for the enormous red and gold neon sign and the perpetual fireworks that splashed across the sky overhead, thanks to some very expensive magework. They were visible in the daytime but truly spectacular at night.

The parking lot was full, as usual. He and Romano let the valet take Dominic's car. Inside, slot machines ka-chinged, waiters glided by with trays of free drinks, and gorgeous, half-naked men and women in gilded cages shifted to animal form and back for an audience of dazzled non-magics.

As they made their way through the casino, Romano trotted along at Dominic's side, a couple of steps behind him. It was a pack hierarchy thing.

The closer they got to Arturo's office, the more the hair stood up on Dominic's neck.

"Something's off," he muttered, glancing back at Romano, who quickened his step so he was right next to Dominic in case of an attack.

"Yeah, I feel it." Romano nodded.

When they reached the door to Arturo's office, a familiar scent drifted into Dominic's nostrils.

The Bianchi Pack? What the hell?

He smelled Primo, Primo's brother and underboss Luigi, and Fabiana.

There was another scent there, one that reeked of magic so strong he had to be a high-level mage. Dominic didn't hear or scent anything that indicated trouble, but still, the Bianchi Pack members had come to the Arena? That was unprecedented. He and Romano barreled into the room, bracing for a fight.

Dominic's gaze swept the room quickly. On the surface, everything was calm. Arturo sat on a throne-like chair in front of a rectangular, hand-carved table with paws for legs—the paws of a rival mob boss.

Even in a crisis, he was cool, unruffled, and elegant. He wore an exquisitely hand-cut raw silk suit the color of gunmetal and tailored to fit his six-feet-five-inch height. He had thick, dark hair with a silver streak through it, and a smile that made wolf pups cry and never seemed to reach his amber eyes.

"Please, join us," he said in a deep, rumbling voice as if it were an actual request rather than an order.

Giuliana sat to his left with Arturo's cousins, Carlo and Ottavio, sitting next to him on the right. Arturo had turned them in the 1950s.

Ottavio was on the same level as Dominic, a *Capo*. Unfortunately, Carlo wasn't. The turn had gone wrong with Carlo, and now the seven-feet-tall murder machine was childlike but still deadly.

At the far end of the table was a dark-haired, narrow-faced man Dominic recognized from news stories. It was Benedict, a member of the Council of Mages. That wasn't a good sign; they only involved themselves in shifter affairs when some major shiznit was going down.

At the opposite side of the table, facing Arturo, were the Bianchis.

Primo and Luigi were big, blocky men dressed in dark suits. They always looked as if they were on their way to a funeral. Fabiana sat between her uncles, melodramatically dabbing at her reddened eyes with a handkerchief. She wore a pink spandex dress that clung to her body like a second skin. When Dominic walked in, she burst into loud, noisy tears and Primo patted her on the arm and glared at Dominic.

"Don't you worry, we will avenge your honor," Primo said loudly.

What the hell?

"What honor?" Romano muttered in a low voice. Dominic elbowed him in the ribs, hard. The situation was already tense enough; he didn't need Romano stirring things up with his smart mouth.

Arturo waved his hand at Romano and Dominic, indicating they should stand next to him.

"You took your time," Primo snarled at Dominic. "No respect. No respect at all."

"You will address me, not my men," Arturo said coldly. "And since this visit was unexpected, you're lucky we even agreed to this meeting."

"Excuse me. I am the mediator, and I will do the talking," Mage Benedict interrupted impatiently.

Arturo nodded gravely. "Proceed."

"I'll cut right to the chase. We are here to address a grievance from the Bianchi Pack," Mage Benedict said to Dominic. "Primo Bianchi states you formally agreed to a mating contract with Fabiana Bianchi, which was intended to help unite your packs and act as a peace offering."

Peace offering, my furry ass.

Several months ago, the Bianchi Pack had restarted the hostilities in the first place by carjacking one of the Moretti Pack's trucks, claiming it had been in their territories. Their actions had set off a revenge raid by the Moretti Pack, and the two packs had been low-key taking shots at each other ever since.

"After agreeing to this, they say you deliberately humiliated her by mate-biting another female right in front of her," Mage Benedict continued in a deeply concerned tone.

At this, Fabiana let out a loud, fake wail and collapsed into her uncle's arms.

Dominic snorted with contempt. "Arturo, you know I would never agree to a mating contract without first seeking your approval and blessing."

Arturo nodded slightly.

Ottavio echoed the gesture with a vigorous nod of his own. "None of us would," he said loudly with a fierce glower at the Bianchi's. Ottavio, who was slavishly devoted to Arturo, was all about pack honor.

Arturo addressed Mage Benedict. "They approached us with the offer several weeks ago, and I said I would consider it. Mating is for life; it is not a decision I would make hastily. As a sign of good faith, I told him I would expect them to refrain from any further attacks on my men and my property while I decided."

"And we did!" Primo snarled. "Because we keep our word. And because Dominic had agreed the mating would take place. Otherwise, why would we have called off our men?"

Dominic turned to Benedict. "I repeat, I did no such thing. Fabiana has sent me texts and tried to call me repeatedly over the past few weeks. I have not answered one call, I have not contacted her, and I was *not* the one who invited her to the party last night either."

"Neither was I," Arturo said, a hint of steel in his voice. "We're not certain how her name got on the guest list."

That wasn't good. The party was at the Royal Palms Banquet Hall, where they held all their pack functions. Had their security been compromised?

"I came because I was invited!" Fabiana whined and looked accusingly at Dominic, blinking her tear-stained eyes. Her mascara hadn't even clumped; Dominic would have bet a million bucks she was wearing waterproof makeup because she had planned the fake waterworks in advance. Hell, she'd probably rehearsed this little scene all morning. "You asked me to come! And you were all over me!"

"Excuse me, I was *what*?" Dominic said incredulously.

At the same time, Giuliana strangled on a laugh.

"You couldn't keep your hands off me!" Fabiana's face flushed in a very convincing display of anger.

"He couldn't get away from you fast enough!" Giuliana laughed so hard, tears ran down her cheeks. Her uncle elbowed her, but his mouth twitched in a brief smile.

Primo growled and let his fangs descend. Luigi leapt to his feet, his face turning furry, and his jaw lengthening. Arturo just sat there with a faint look of amused disdain. To not even bother to react was the ultimate show of disrespect.

"Enough!" Benedict snapped, and Primo and Luigi settled down while Fabiana sniveled quietly and daintily dabbed at her eyes with a tissue. "Who was in charge of the guest list?"

"I was." Giuliana's smooth brow wrinkled in a frown. "The guest list was printed out from the computer. It is possible it was an error because Fabiana was at the last two parties. I went over the list myself before the party, though, and I'm sure she wasn't on it. Perhaps an old list was printed out instead."

Dominic thought an error sounded unlikely, and he could see it in Arturo's face too.

What would somebody have to gain by sneaking her into the party?

Dominic cleared his throat loudly and leaned forward. "Even if I had agreed to the mating, *which I did not,* a mate-bite on a full moon supersedes that unless I had already bitten and bonded with Fabiana, which would eradicate my ability to sense my true mate. When a wolf spots his mate on the full moon and marks her as his, any prior agreements are nullified. It has been this way throughout history. This is understood by all shifter packs, including the Bianchis. We honor the instincts of our wolves."

Benedict glanced at Primo and arched an eyebrow. "Is that true?"

Primo scowled. "It's not as universal as they're claiming."

"Bullshit," Giuliana coughed into her hand, earning her a sharp look from her uncle and a snarl from Luigi.

Benedict heaved a sigh. "I will have to consult with Jeremiah."

Jeremiah was the Mage Council's shifter consultant. He was a member of the Moonstone Pack. They owned the family entertainment area in the south side of Encantado and were considered neutral when it came to the fight between the Bianchis and the Moretti Pack. They liked to present themselves as respectable businessmen, although plenty of their guys liked to sneak into the dirtier parts of town to sample their wares.

"I will be in touch. You will not take any further action until I give you my decision. And now I would like to speak to Arturo alone."

The Bianchi Pack members stood, making a big production of it by loudly shoving their chairs back. Fabiana pretended to half-swoon, and Primo propped her up as they stomped out of the room.

"My God," Giuliana said in wonder. "She should be on a telenovela. I almost wanted to ask for her autograph."

"Surely, you didn't fall for her act, Benedict" Arturo said impatiently. "They're trying to start a war because they hope to take over our territory. Plain and simple."

Benedict shrugged. "She was obviously camping it up, but that doesn't settle the question of whether the Bianchi Pack has been wronged."

He drummed his fingers on the table and gave Dominic a speculative look. "So the mating claim is official? You have brought her back to the pack territory?"

Dominic shook his head. "No, tradition states she does not have to return here until the next full moon."

Arturo nodded.

What Dominic didn't add was the reason for the tradition. If a warrior-class shifter bit a non-wolf, she would very likely not survive the bite. Waiting to bring her back to the pack territory allowed her time to say farewell to friends and family.

Dominic's fur prickled under his skin at the thought. That wouldn't happen to Zoey. The serum would protect her—his fierce, adorable Zoey, who amusingly thought she could escape him even though she didn't really want to. His wolf itched to be with her already. It didn't understand why he couldn't just grab her by the nape of her neck and drag her back home with him.

"In that case, you could still marry Fabiana and unite the two packs." Benedict mused. "It would avoid a potential war."

"You disrespect our traditions," Arturo growled, baring his fangs. "The wolf made its claim."

"Very well. We will notify you as soon as we make a decision," Benedict replied, his dark brows drawing together.

Anger swelled in Dominic's chest. There shouldn't be any debate.

Benedict stood to leave. "One more thing. We've had our first ghoul sighting in years. A human couple was camping in Scorched Earth, and they barely escaped."

Giuliana's eyes grew wide. "What were they doing at Scorched Earth?"

Scorched Earth was an area north of the city, near the Portal. A dragon had flown out of the portal a couple of years ago and burned down a wide swath of pine forest before the combined power of the city's most powerful mages took it down.

"They were filming themselves, hoping to be on one of those reality T.V. shows."

"Ugh." Giuliana wrinkled her nose, although Dominic knew keeping up with a certain T.V. family was her guilty pleasure.

"Did they actually see the ghouls?" Arturo raised a brow.

Benedict shook his head. "No, or they probably wouldn't have survived to tell. Their dog went crazy barking and alerted them. As they ran for their car, the wind shifted and they smelled the ghouls," he said. "They called the police as soon as they got back in cell phone range. The police's sniffer officers found ghoul footprints and ghoul scent."

Dominic wrinkled his nose in disgust; ghouls smelled foul.

"The ghouls walked to a river and the scent disappeared," Benedict concluded.

"Did the dog get away?" Carlo blurted out, and everyone turned to look at him.

"Yes," Benedict said, flashing him an irritated look. "The dog was right at their heels when they fled."

"Oh, good. I like dogs." Carlo didn't seem to notice Benedict's annoyance.

Ottavio elbowed his brother, who just looked at him in confusion.

Dominic felt a chill of unease.

Zoey's neighborhood was pretty far north. Of course, there were guard stations all across the city's northern border, dedicated to keeping any magic spillover away from the city.

One bite from a ghoul was fatal to humans, and mages too for that matter. Within minutes, the bitten turned to mindless, rage-filled husks of their former selves. The fact shifters were immune to the effects of a ghoul bite was one reason they were so vital to the city's defense.

Dominic saw the look on Arturo's face. Ghouls walking to a river? It almost sounded as if they'd done that so they could wade in the water and throw off the trackers. That would indicate planning. Intelligence. If there were some new type of ghoul spilling out of the portal, the type with the ability to reason, then humanity was hosed.

"They couldn't have come through the portal." Arturo tapped his fingers on the table, his thick brows drawing together. "The guards would have reported it."

"Yes, I know," Benedict acknowledged. "No ghouls have emerged from the main portal. There's always the possibility of a lesser portal having opened."

At least lesser portals never stayed open long. It was unheard of for them to be open for more than a few hours.

Arturo's gaze never flickered. "I can put my best scenters on it. Maybe they can pick up something the police missed."

"That would be appreciated. Have them report to our headquarters." Benedict nodded at Arturo and the others and left.

Ottavio waited until he was gone before spinning on Dominic with a snarl. "Your wolf just had to bite her, didn't it?"

"Yes," Dominic snapped, "it did. Would you like to discuss the matter further?" By which he meant, did he want Dominic to slice him, dice him, and make his fur into a coat?

Romano let out a low, rumbling growl of support but hung back.

Ottavio leapt to his feet, face going furry, and Dominic followed suit, waiting for an attack order.

"Enough!" Arturo barked, and they were blasted with a wave of energy which froze them on the spot. "I have enough to deal with. I don't need to watch you assholes having a dick measuring contest."

"Ow!" Giuliana squealed. The energy wasn't directed at her, but anyone close to Arturo would feel the spillover.

Every muscle in Dominic's body was locked in place, and his lungs were on fire. Spots swam in front of his eyes. Ottavio's face turned purple.

Arturo, as Alpha, drew on the power of the entire pack and used it when he deemed necessary. He could force shifters to change to animal or human form, or freeze them in place, which was agonizing and could be deadly if he kept his hold on them long enough.

When Arturo released them, they both staggered back, gasping for breath.

Arturo's voice battered them. "Ottavio, we don't control the moon-bite of our wolves; it is one of our most sacred traditions. And Dominic, Ottavio is speaking out of loyalty to me and concern for the pack. This matter is settled. Let it go."

Dominic and Ottavio nodded and inclined their heads to the side, exposing their throats. To appear submissive like this was excruciating. It shredded at Dominic's wolf and made it howl with pain and rage inside. Arturo knew that, of course; it was part of their punishment.

He glared at them and finally nodded. They both raised their heads and took a step back.

Arturo's cold gaze swept over them. "Both of you need to watch your backs. The Bianchi Pack is making it clear they'll do anything to provoke a war. Put the word out."

Dominic nodded, feeling a swell of frustration. Normally, he'd be chomping at the bit for a good pack war, but he needed time to woo Zoey and show her he could be a good mate.

Once he and Romano had left the room, he turned on his subordinate with a growl.

"You started going furry back there. Don't," Dominic bit out through gritted teeth.

"Just didn't like the way he was talking to you." Romano shot a dirty look over his shoulder.

"You think I need you to fight my battles for me? You think I need you to make me look weak?"

A look of shock crossed Romano's face but vanished instantly.

"I know you have my back. I appreciate it," Dominic said, tamping down his temper. His craving for Zoey was making him snappish. Now that his wolf had bitten her, it wanted her by his side immediately. The memory of her sweet scent tantalized his nostrils and flooded his brain with images of her soft, curvy body tangled up in his sheets. And in his arms.

Romano nodded, his face serious. "My wolf just reacts. That's how we're wired." He grimaced. "I didn't mean it like …"

Romano was a born wolf. He was closer to his animal than Dominic ever would be. If Dominic had pups—*when* Zoey gave him pups—they'd be like Romano in that way. Made wolves were considered lesser by some, lower in prestige. He didn't want that for his pups.

"It's fine." Dominic shrugged. "I'll be on edge until Zoey's part of the pack."

It wasn't just his craving that had him ready to bite off heads. The fact his wolf was taking to Zoey so strongly was both a blessing and a source of guilt. His wolf had once craved another.

Is it wrong for me to want to feel something again?

A face from long ago swam in front of him, and he was ashamed because that face had blurred with time and he couldn't bring it back into focus.

CHAPTER *Four*

With a few hours of sleep under her belt, Zoey marched over to the apartment of her neighbor Danielle, a water witch and friend of hers. Danielle was on the neighborhood improvement committee with Zoey, and she worked the night shift at the utilities department.

On a power scale of one to ten, she was about a two on a good day. She could cause extremely small areas of rain or widespread mist. "Too early," Danielle groaned, standing in the doorway in her pajamas. Her pre-noon crankiness matched Zoey's cheerfulness in equal measure. "Go away, Satan's alarm clock."

"Ooh, good one. But it's late afternoon. We have to talk about Monday's meeting. Everyone's meeting us at Mary's. I will coffee you until you're human again."

The local business owners and community leaders had agreed to meet with their committee to talk about the garbage problem.

"Fiiiiine. Give me five minutes to get dressed, horrible wench-face," Danielle mumbled, and Zoey waited at the door until Danielle returned wearing jeans, calf-high boots, and a light-blue sweater. She grumbled all the way to Mary's Diner, so Zoey kept up a line of cheerful patter about the lovely weather, just to annoy her.

Stewart and Andrea—other members of the committee—were waiting for them as they rounded the corner to Mary's Meetinghouse.

Andrea's tall, skinny, and sullen teenaged son Lorenzo stood next to his mother with his hands shoved in the pockets of his jeans.

Stewart was a carpenter who owned a small shop down the block from Zoey's apartment building. His white mop of hair and round, gold-rimmed glasses made him look older than his fifty-something years. Andrea, a gawky brunette in her forties, was a graphic designer. She'd moved with her son to Encantado when they'd discovered Lorenzo was a fire wizard with just enough power to light candles. Her husband had reacted differently—he'd promptly filed for divorce.

The windows to the building were boarded up, the magical anti-burglar runes nailed over the doorway were no longer glowing, and there was a "closed for business" sign on the front door.

"Seriously," Danielle said, staring at the shop. "This can't be, and yet it is. You know what fuels my perky Pollyanna personality?"

Zoey gave her a sidelong glance. "Say what?" She looked at Andrea. "Have I missed something?"

"Caffeine," Danielle said miserably. "That's what makes me human. Do you see what I see? A caffeine desert."

"Perky Pollyanna personality. That's a lot of Ps in one sentence," Zoey said to Danielle. "So are you now a crabby, caffeine-deprived crumpet?"

"Nothing is funny until I get coffee. What gives? Why does this keep happening to me? I mean, to us," Danielle groaned. "But mostly me."

Zoey shook her head. "No idea. I was in there two days ago and they didn't say anything about closing up."

Another one. A ghost of uneasiness whispered through her. Why were so many businesses in her neighborhood folding? Did they know something she didn't?

"Maybe it's the trash?" Stewart shrugged.

"We live in a trashy neighborhood, all right," Stewart said.

Zoey and Dominique let out obligatory groans. Stewart prided himself on his painfully bad puns. Andrea giggled. Lorenzo rolled his eyes and started to walk away.

Andrea's smiled faded. "Where are you going?" she called out after him.

"Home!"

"Don't go anywhere else! Go straight home, and don't stop off anywhere!" Andrea yelled as he vanished around the corner.

Zoey felt a twinge of sympathy. Being a single mom with a surly teenaged son would be challenging enough. In a city where hanging out with the wrong crowd might end up with being reduced to spare parts for a witch's brew, it would have to be a twenty on a stress-scale of one to ten.

"It's not like there are no customers for these businesses. People still need to eat," Andrea pointed out, looking at the closed-up café and shaking her head. "They still need to shop."

"Yeah, that's true. All right, the closest coffee shop is Big Betty's. Twenty blocks," Danielle moaned. "Screw everything in the world."

They trooped off down the block, heading west.

"At least it's a nice day," Zoey said. "Sunny, no clouds, and the breeze is currently carrying the scent of garbage away from us."

"Thanks for the weather report. By the way, why are you walking funny?" Danielle yawned. "Hot date last night?"

A blush burned Zoey's cheeks. "Ha ha, you're hilarious. I had a catering gig."

"Oh, right. So you didn't end up romping with any of the party guests?"

Zoey summoned an expression of outrage. "I am a professional!"

"That doesn't really answer my question. And your face is turning kinda red. Why are you walking like that?" Danielle persisted.

Stewart and Andrea were looking at her with interest now.

There is no easy way to say "A werewolf bit me on the ass last night, and now he says I'm going to be his mate at the next full moon. But then he didn't like the way I kissed, so he left me. I think."

"Pulled a muscle," Zoey lied.

"You should get that looked at," Andrea said. "The witch doctor over on Twelfth is open weekends."

Can a witch doctor treat a werewolf bite?

Anyway, Zahara the witch doctor was ungodly expensive, so it would have to wait.

"All right, we need a proposal for the neighborhood meeting Monday night," Zoey announced, changing the subject.

Danielle looked gloomy. "I don't know. Sometimes it feels like it's pointless."

"That's the lack of caffeine speaking," Zoey assured her. "Fine, I won't ask you again until after I've poured a double-shot latte down your throat."

They made it to the coffee shop. Andrea ordered pastry for everyone because that was what she did—she fed people. She and Zoey were a good team. When they held neighborhood meetings, Zoey cheered everyone up, and Andrea worried about people and fussed over them like she was everyone's mom, not just Lorenzo's. Danielle was actually a hard worker who hustled a lot, despite her constant grumbling.

They settled down at a round table painted like a Ouija board, and then nobody talked until Danielle had finished her second cup of coffee. Except for Stewart mildly mentioning the coffee shop was full of "has-beans." He had to spell it out to explain what he meant, and everyone groaned except for Andrea who laughed kindly because she always had to encourage people, even the world's worst punner.

"Okay, guys," Danielle finally said, "we have no way to get mass amounts of garbage out of this neighborhood. What are we gonna do, take little baggies of it to the business district and drop it in the public trash cans on the street? That would take a million years; we'd never get ahead. I mean, it's hopeless, right?"

Zoey was the kind of person who heard "hopeless" and made it into a personal challenge. Leaning back in her chair, her eyes traveled the room and landed on the three garbage cans in the corner.

"Compost," Zoey said suddenly. "How did I not think of that before?'

Danielle looked at her in confusion. "Compost?"

"Compost, and community vegetable gardens." Zoey started warming to the idea. "There are so many empty lots. We can start organizing volunteer teams to bring the trash to designated lots and use some of the overflowing dumpsters as compost bins. Yes, it's going to be a gross job, but no worse than walking down our streets these days. If I spend some time in the community vegetable gardens, they'll grow like crazy. I'm like fertilizer."

Danielle went to fetch herself more coffee. "You realize you just basically called yourself a pile of manure?" she said when she returned.

"Yes, but let's run with it."

"I think it's a brilliant idea," Andrea said enthusiastically. "Don't you, Stewart?"

"Absolutely." He bobbed his head. If Andrea had said the sky was purple and the streets were made of taffy, he'd have agreed with that too.

They all looked at Danielle. Danielle took a very long, dramatic sip of coffee, paused for effect, and finally set her mug on the table. "It's not completely crazy," she replied grudgingly.

"Woot! Coming from you, that's high praise, cranky witch." Zoey smiled.

"And Danielle could make sure the gardens got enough water since she's a wet blanket. Get it, wet blanket? Because she's cranky and also a water witch?" Stewart threw back his head and laughed. Andrea joined him, and Stewart beamed with delight.

Danielle narrowed her eyes. "He's lucky I don't waste good caffeine, or he'd be wearing this," she said to Zoey, holding up her mug. "Give me strength."

Andrea rubbed her hands together happily. "All right, we can present this to the committee on Monday. I'll find out what empty lots we can use."

Andrea went to use the bathroom, and Stewart watched her with a wistful expression.

"You could ask her out, you know," Zoey said.

Stewart's ever-present smile faded. "I have. I guess the timing's not right."

Probably because of Lorenzo. He was about all Andrea could handle right now.

A few minutes later, they were all finished with their coffee and Zoey headed back to her apartment. Suddenly, her map sense flared and a big, blaring "obstacle" warning pounded in her head. The obstacle's sudden appearance almost certainly meant something, or someone, had just spotted her and planned to intercept her. Otherwise, her map magic would have warned her about it earlier.

They were in her neighborhood's business district, on a street lined with shops and restaurants. She glanced around but didn't see any obvious threats. Had one of the Moretti Pack come to grab her?

She elbowed her way through a knot of warlock hipsters on a corner, earning her dirty looks from skinny men with tight jeans and man buns. Ignoring them, she hurried down the next block and quickly dodged down an alleyway, but the pounding of footsteps told her that her pursuer was on her heels.

She slid behind a dumpster, praying she wouldn't be spotted—the alley was a dead end.

CHAPTER FIVE

Loud, thudding footsteps were headed toward Zoey. Anger and fear swirled inside her, rising up and making her reckless. Someone—or something—wanted a piece of her? Fine, she'd make sure they choked on it.

She stomped out from behind the dumpster, fists clenched and ready to punch a hole in something.

And then she grimaced in disgust. The man who'd been following her was Jordan.

He served as the neighborhood liaison for the Moretti Pack since none of the pack members would be caught dead in a run-down neighborhood like this. Jordan made a very nice living working for them. He dressed his short, rotund form in silvery sharkskin suits that were so shiny they looked like tinfoil, and he liked to flash his Rolex.

For some reason, that made Zoey think of Dominic. Like the other high-ranking members of the pack, he was always dressed to the nines. His suits were exquisitely tailored to his muscular body, but they didn't shout for attention the way Jordan's did. They didn't need to. Dominic commanded attention just by strolling into a room with his animal grace and his piercing blue eyes.

Why was she even thinking of him? He'd changed his mind and she didn't have to worry about him anymore, right?

"Zoey!" Jordan leered, sliding in front of her. "Trying to avoid me?"

"Why would I ever?" she said drily. She quickly sidestepped him so he was no longer between her and the end of the alley.

"You haven't paid your share this week." That's what they called the extortion money.

She dug into her purse and reluctantly handed over almost all the tips she'd earned the night before. She'd left forty dollars tucked in her sock. He needed to see her empty her wallet before he'd be satisfied, the greedy bastard. He seemed to get a sick thrill out of separating people from the last of their money.

"Seriously," Zoey said irritably, gesturing at the trash, "What are we paying for? We can't go on like this."

"You got a problem with the way I run things? Maybe you'd like to move to another neighborhood," he snapped.

She glowered at him. He knew she wouldn't. She'd taken on responsibilities here, and she prided herself on being someone who followed through with her promises.

"Thought so," he gloated. "Now, show me your tits and I'll knock a hundred off next week's share." He flashed his big teeth in a loathsome smile.

Zoey instinctively recoiled. She could actually feel her lady-bits shriveling up and trying to tuck themselves inside her body. "Say that again, I'll knock your veneers down your throat."

His face scrunched up like an angry baby's. "Just for that, a hundred-dollar fine for the noise complaint."

"Noise complaint?" Like anybody could hear anything from her apartment with the nightclub pounding away downstairs. "From whom?"

"Me. From the noise you make when you flap your gums." His mouth twisted in an ugly snarl.

"Worth it," she taunted him. "And I have thirty days to appeal the complaint." Zoey walked away as quickly as she could with her butt-cheek still aching. She could feel Jordan's gaze slithering over her backside, and it made her want to take another shower.

As she made her way down the sidewalk, her spell phone rang, the ringtone indicating it was her mother. She sighed. She'd need to stop at the spellectricity store to recharge soon.

She sent a text saying she was at work and she'd call her mother back later, and no, she had not been crisped by a dragon or eaten by a troll.

She was still kind of worried about the Moretti Pack problem, and she wasn't great at lying to her mother over the phone. Her mother would definitely have heard the stress in her voice. Her parents were already completely freaked that their oldest daughter now lived in a portal city.

Of course, they could have moved to Encantado if they chose.

Zoey would never have asked that of them though. She had three brothers and a sister, the youngest of whom was twelve. Life in a portal city was too volatile.

Her parents worried from a distance while Zoey tried to play up the positive aspects of being in Encantado.

She sent them spell phone pictures of fairies flittering in gardens and phoenixes flying overhead, trailing fire, and made it sound as if she lived in a magical wonderland. Often enough, that was true, although she made sure she only snapped those photos when she was in the nicer neighborhoods so her parents wouldn't see the backdrop of graffiti, smashed windows, and trash.

As she walked, her spell phone rang again. If she kept ignoring it, her mother would just get more and more worked up. She stifled a groan and answered with a bright, fake "Hi! Sorry I haven't been in touch! So, yeah, I'm about to deliver a package and ... ouch!"

She'd gotten too close to the apartment building on the corner, and the gargoyle guardian had spat a pebble at her. The building owners fed him a regular diet of sand, and in return, he discouraged intruders.

"What's that?" her mother said suspiciously.

"It's noth– Ouch, ouch, ouch!" Zoey dodged the furious little imp. She made the mistake of picking up a pebble and throwing it back at him. Yeah, like that would hurt a stone guardian. He responded with a machine gun barrage of tiny pea gravel sprayed right at her head.

She ran off shrieking, dodging around a corner, and then realized her mother was still on the phone.

"Fine! I'm fine! Everything is fine!"

"What is happening?" her mother cried out. "Oh Lord, are you being eaten by one of those phoenix things?"

"What? Phoenixes are vegetarians!" she said, hurrying toward her apartment building. "I'm fine. I just sprained my ankle. Really, Mom, I'll call you back tomorrow. Loveyabye!" Zoey hung up quickly.

"Move to an enchanted city, they said," she muttered under her breath as she stomped up the stairs. "It'll be magical, they said."

She grabbed a bicycle and headed back downstairs. Twenty minutes later, she rolled to a stop in front of an old warehouse building. It was currently the residence of an ever-changing crew of homeless teenagers. Most of them, like her, were magical anomalies who'd been forced to relocate to a portal city. Outside of magic zones, it seemed to happen on average about one every million births.

The warehouse was old, and its busted windows stared out at the street like rows of dark, angry eyes. Weeds choked the parking lot in front. Lorenzo and his two friends, Cin and Heath, were sitting on plastic crates, watching a sullen goth spray-paint enormous dongs on the warehouse wall.

Lorenzo was smoking a cigarette; that was new. Zoey wheeled her bicycle right up next to him and gave him a look, and he quickly dropped it and squashed it under the heel of his sneaker.

"Don't tell my mom," he said.

"His *mom*," Cin scoffed. She was a skinny little thing with spiky blue hair. She had some kind of magic ability, but she wouldn't say what it was. Her hobbies were shoplifting, making snarky comments, and … yeah, that was about it.

"Great." Lorenzo scowled at the ground, embarrassed. He was still basically a good kid, but Zoey was afraid he wouldn't be for much longer. He'd dropped out of the tech school where he'd been majoring in computer programming, even though he was really good at it. Now he spent his free time hanging out with this group of low-level criminals. Sooner or later, he'd find himself in real trouble, and that would break Andrea's heart.

"Hey, it's a beautiful day to go dumpster diving!" Zoey said in her most cheerful voice.

She made time to take the local kids dumpster diving a couple times a week. If they had food and stayed busy, they'd have less time to make mischief. Due to her map magic, she could guide them to the dumpsters behind the high-end grocery stores in the better neighborhoods and avoid security guards, random guard gargoyles, and other nuisances.

Cin shrugged. "I guess," she said, but she leapt to her feet with an eagerness that belied her bored-with-the-world tone.

She waited while they fetched their battered bicycles, and then they followed her south.

The beat-up warehouses and half-empty buildings gave way to small, shabby ranch houses with cheap protection wards glowing next to their front doors. In some cases, the glow had faded, which meant they hadn't been recharged.

As they kept peddling south, those houses gave way to larger houses, mostly Mediterranean-style with barrel-tile roofs or adobe houses with massive stucco walls. The yards were trimmed and artfully splattered with flowerbeds. The houses here had entire rows of wards up and down the sides of front doors and underneath the windows, and they glowed with their full magical charge. There were house Gargoyles perched on the rooftops and enchanted stone lions at the ends of driveways.

The heads of the stone lions slowly turned and watched them with their blank eyes as they pedaled by.

Finally, a half-hour later, they were in a nice shopping district. They didn't circle around to the front of the stores. There wasn't a single thing any of them could afford, and their mere appearance tended to attract the attention of shifter bodyguards.

They glided down back alleyways until they reached their destination—Le Gourmand. Zoey felt badly about letting Lorenzo come because he was supposed to be home. At least he wasn't out spray-painting a building or boosting cigarettes in an effort to impress Cin.

The dumpster behind Le Gourmand made the trip worthwhile. They found bags of apples, bags of oranges, day-old French bread, and bags of donuts. The owners of Le Gourmand were pretty considerate, and when they threw away expired food, they tried to make sure it was in good enough shape to be used by those who needed it.

"This is great!" Cin crowed, hugging a bag of food to her chest. She glanced at Lorenzo and said in a low voice, "I'm sorry I made fun of you earlier. It must be nice to still have a mom." She always put on the tough badass act, but a little sweetness seeped through on occasion.

"No big." Lorenzo shrugged, trying to look casual, but a smile tugged at his lips.

When the kids' bags were full, Zoey closed her eyes, pictured the route home, and suddenly sensed obstacles. Several of them. She shook her head, trying to refocus, but every route felt blocked.

Too bad her map magic wouldn't tell her what was in her way. Somehow, though, she had the feeling the obstacles were specific to her.

"Guys," she said, "we need to split up. There's something between us and our neighborhood. Can you hang out here for a little while? I'm going to try to find a way back. Just wait a half-hour or so and you should be fine."

She chose a route that took her through a witch suburb, which was always kind of fun because she got to pass by covens practicing their spells in their front yards.

It was nighttime when she glided to a stop in front of her building. A delivery van was idling at the curb, and a man stood by her door with a huge crystal vase full of peonies.

Dominic. But how did he know peonies were her favorite?

"Zoey Monroe?" the man said as she eyed him warily.

"She skipped out on her rent and left town. You're lucky you missed her. She was a major twatmuffin." She quickly sidestepped him, wheeling her bike.

He moved between her and her front door. "He said you'd say that."

"He said I'd say Zoey skipped out on her rent and was a twatmuffin?" she said skeptically. "That's awfully specific."

"He said you'd give me some smartass answer and say you weren't her. You look like the picture he showed me."

Dominic had a picture of her? Yikes.

The delivery man shoved the vase of flowers into her arms and stood back, waiting.

"What else?" Zoey said impatiently.

"You got a tip for me?"

"Yeah, avoid Main Street; the traffic is murder right now."

He gave her a look most people reserve for times when they've stepped in something smelly. She ignored him and maneuvered her way awkwardly to her front door, wheeling her bike with the vase tucked under her arm.

The protection wards over the doorway recognized her, and the lock clicked open. Reluctantly, she set the vase down in the lobby. They were beautiful, but she wasn't taking a gift from someone whose pack was responsible for mountain-high garbage piles clogging up her streets.

Upstairs in her apartment, Zoey plopped down on the couch to try to figure out what to do next. Dominic was sending her flowers. At her apartment. And he had a picture of her.

All those times she'd yearned for a man who actually made her feel desirable and sexy and worth pursuing? She could never have dreamed up a scenario like this. She didn't even know what was going on right now. She didn't know where Dominic lived, what he specifically did for a living, or what he was like as a person. What would it mean to be the mate of a Moretti *Capo*? Most of the parties she'd catered had been attended by single men. She knew this because married pack members wore a chunky gold wedding ring with two wolves side by side.

She had catered one family event for them in the tourist area. Strictly PG. It had been a birthday party for the six-year-old twin pups of a high-ranking pack member. The wives were beautiful, perfectly made up, and exquisitely dressed.

She had to admit the women all had seemed to be happy. Were they putting on a show? Did the women feel they'd sold their souls by marrying into a crime family? If so, they didn't make it obvious.

She'd been surprised at how tender the big, fierce daddy wolves had been with their children. She felt a sudden stab of longing as she remembered a big, scarred wolf gently scooping up his little pup after the child had scraped his knees.

I want that. I want that for my children, a man who will adore them and protect them and comfort them

She'd dated so many losers who'd tried to make her feel like she should be grateful for any scrap of attention. On some very deep level, she'd started to doubt she'd ever have a good relationship.

But did she want it with Dominic?

Or, more importantly, did she want it with a Moretti wolf? It was a package deal. She couldn't have one without the other.

And she couldn't make such an enormous, life-changing decision based on the fact Dominic's wolf apparently thought she had a tasty butt.

How far would Dominic go to claim her? He'd insisted she was going to be his mate. Would he kidnap her and haul her back to pack property? She didn't know what the pack mating rituals consisted of, but she wasn't taking any chances.

Zoey quickly packed up some clothes and climbed back on her bike. Her legs were starting to ache, and it was late evening now, but she headed downtown, to the business district. The owner of the bike messenger service had a few tiny studio apartments in the building next to the dispatch center and allowed the employees to crash there if they wanted to pick up some early jobs the next day.

CHAPTER Six

"I don't suppose you'd care to tell me where you are?" Kalinda said when Zoey called her Sunday morning.

Zoey picked up on the hidden meaning in her boss's words. Kalinda's calls were being monitored—by the Moretti Pack.

"Oh, here, there, and everywhere. By the way, what did you mean when you told Dominic there were other girls who would be better suited for him?"

"You heard that?" Zoey could feel Kalinda's wince all the way through the phone.

"Yes. Because I have ears."

"Oh, you know. Flashier. Trashier. The type they usually like."

"Skinnier?"

"Oh, come on." But Kalinda didn't say no.

Zoey scowled and let an uncomfortable silence drag out.

"I was trying to help you," Kalinda said defensively. "Those mafia shifters tend to be the lusty types, so for their events, I hire waitresses who are less likely to be harassed by those guys. Most of them like magazine model types with hair extensions, spell-enhanced tans, and fake bazoongas. That is not you. Is that so bad?"

"Whatever," Zoey said, stung. "So ... I guess I can't work any gigs for you in the near future?"

"Well, if you did, I am under orders to report back to the Moretti Pack immediately. And I would never disobey a pack order." Kalinda's voice was brisk and business-like.

"Got it. See you around." Zoey hung up without saying goodbye because her feelings were hurt.

It was mildly chilly on Sunday morning, and Zoey sensed more obstacles than usual as she zipped through the streets delivering packages.

The bite wound still ached, making the ride really awkward. Between the obstacles and the bite, she was much slower than usual, which meant she was only slightly quicker than an average bike messenger.

When she finished her deliveries around noon, she headed back to her tiny crash pad. When she got to the hallway, she stopped. She smelled coffee. She hadn't made coffee this morning. In fact, there was no coffee in the little apartment. No food either. She waited a few minutes before finally heading in. What were the odds someone would make coffee for her and then kill her?

Hopefully not good.

Dominic was sitting on the tiny couch-bed as she limped through the door of the apartment. He wore a suit, as usual—a nice charcoal-gray. There was now a coffeemaker filled with coffee sitting on the kitchen counter. A smile curled his sensual mouth as she shut the door behind her. Her heart stuttered in her chest. From fear or anticipation? She wasn't sure.

His gaze swept the little living room/bedroom. "Hello. Nice place you've got here."

"Well, it smells better than my actual neighborhood," she said irritably. He looked mildly puzzled at that and held out a cup of coffee.

"Yes, that's what happens when you don't pay your dues."

Seriously? He was going to pretend the neighborhood wasn't paying? She gave him a sour look. "Whatever helps you sleep at night."

Zoey limped over to Dominic, her butt aching with every step, and grudgingly accepted the cup of coffee.

She made sure to sit on the far end of the small couch. Unfortunately, it wasn't far enough. There was maybe six inches of space between them, and the warmth of his gaze made the apartment feel stifling. She could practically feel the lust waves rolling off him. Or was it her?

She took a sip of coffee. He made a mean cup of java, she had to admit. Smooth and delicious. Just like him.

"If this whole mobster thing doesn't work out for you, you'd make a kickass barista."

He stifled a chuckle.

"What?"

His voice was deep and gravelly as he studied her with an amused look. "Most people don't give me grief because they're too afraid of me."

She took another sip. "Put me in the 'really annoyed' category instead, thanks."

"I like how you banter. You're funny. I think I'll keep you."

She wasn't going to dignify that with an answer. "What brings you around here? Slumming?"

"Nope." He shifted on the couch, angling his body toward hers, and the furniture groaned under his weight. "I came to help you out. I could be a real asshole and let you keep limping around, or I could tell you how to heal that bite."

She stared at him, her eyes narrowing. "And then kidnap me?"

"Nope. I'm just going to court the living hell out of you until you smarten up and realize what you're missing."

"I don't think your lifespan is actually going to be that long. But anyway, back to healing my butt …"

He stood, and the couch shifted again. "When a werewolf bites his female, the only thing that heals the pain is his saliva. He has to shift back to human form and … use his tongue. If you'd stuck around after I bit you, I would have healed you."

"Seriously? You thought I'd stick around after that?" she spluttered indignantly.

Dominic smiled. "You'll learn. You miss out on all kinds of good things by running away from me."

Zoey looked up him. He towered over her, his muscular arms folded across his broad chest, and he wasn't budging.

Was she seriously considering this?

"Turn your back. And don't try anything funny," she warned him, which for some reason made him chuckle. Ha ha, she was a laugh riot today.

She stood and quickly stripped down to her bra and underwear, telling herself it was just because she needed to be able to walk again without limping. That was the only reason she was alone in an apartment, in her skivvies, with the sexiest man she'd ever seen—the man who'd claimed her as his bride.

Definitely.

Totally.

So why were her nipples pebbling with desire? Why were her panties damp?

Zoey closed her eyes and tried to remind herself why she wouldn't give in to him. She pictured mountains of garbage and scampering rats. Steering her bike around dead bodies on the sidewalk in the business district—or rather, pieces of dead bodies. A Moretti signature.

She felt the soft caress of his tongue dragging down her right butt cheek and forgot to think. All she could do was feel. It felt like velvet gliding across her aching flesh, and the pain faded instantly.

"Better?" Dominic's husky voice stroked her like a lover's caress.

She turned around.

He was still kneeling, and he was dangerously close. He grabbed her hips, holding her in place as he tenderly kissed her stomach—her soft stomach with the fold that lapped over the top of her panties. She sucked in a breath.

"Don't," he said sternly.

"Don't what?"

"Don't try to make yourself less than you are. I want all of you. Every delicious inch."

She tried to step backward, but he held her still while he kissed her panties—just the outside.

"I won't settle for anything less, Zoey," he growled.

God, that is the sexiest thing anyone has ever said to me.

"You are not the boss off me." Zoey's legs trembled.

"Ha! That's a good one. I like you, princess. I haven't laughed this much in ages." He grabbed her panties with his teeth and tugged them down. "You can tell me to stop anytime you want to." He pressed his face into her damp curls. She kept them neatly trimmed, a close-clipped golden-brown triangle.

"I-I can?"

"Yes." He breathed in deeply as if inhaling fragrant roses. The hot wave of desire that washed over her nearly made her collapse. "Here. Your knees seem a little weak."

He sprang to his feet and moved her back to the couch. Such a gentleman. So helpful. Somehow, she stepped out of her panties while he did that. Accidentally.

Her knees couldn't hold her up anymore, and she sank down onto the couch, legs quivering. "I can tell you to stop whenever I want?"

He knelt in front of her and slid his hands between her legs, roughly spreading them apart.

"Yes." He nipped her thigh gently, and a jolt of pleasurable pain pulsed through her body. "But you won't."

Her legs quivered, and he pressed harder, spreading them wider. She was completely exposed to him. His warm breath fanned her sex, and he breathed in again, inhaling her scent. She could tell him to stop. She was going to tell him, any second now …

But what would it feel like to have his eager tongue lapping at her? Probing her aching pussy, sucking on the swollen pink pearl of her clit?

Footsteps pounded up the stairs, and Zoey leapt to her feet, her body crying out in protest. Dominic let out a stream of curses. Quickly, she snatched her t-shirt and pants and pulled them back on. She kicked the underwear under the couch just as someone rapped loudly on the door.

"Boss, it's me! Arturo called. Said you'd turned off your phone."

The door swung open, and Romano stepped into the room. Zoey stood there shivering with mingled desire and fury. Dammit, she'd been one lick away from climbing Dominic like a tree and begging him to take her.

Dominic looked at Romano with murder in his icy blue eyes.

"I knew it was you, idiot. I could scent you," he growled. "Eat less garlic. And I told you to *wait out front*. If you've got a death wish, though, I'm happy to oblige. Evisceration, decapitation? Or a good old-fashioned flaying?"

"Why is she giving me a dirty look?" Romano, looking wounded, ignored Dominic's threats. "I didn't eat her friend the other day. Did you guys finish having sex yet? Arturo needs you."

"We didn't have sex!" Zoey squawked indignantly.

"Okay. Sure. I don't know what sex smells like." Romano gave her an exaggerated wink. He glanced down at her pink panties which were half peeking out from under the couch. Looking at her again, he stuck his hands in his pockets and started whistling. Loudly. On purpose.

"*Why are you here?!*" Dominic shouted so loudly the room shook and Zoey's eardrums popped as if she were in an airplane.

"Check your spell phone. Arturo's got a job for you."

Dominic pulled his phone from his jacket pocket. He read the screen, sighed, and shook his head. "Unfortunately, I've got to go kill a guy," he said, tucking the phone back into his pocket.

Zoey looked at him in shock.

He shrugged. "You might as well know what your mate does for a living."

"Why are you killing him?" Her voice came out all squeaky.

There was no trace of seduction left in his face. He gave her a blank look as if she'd started speaking Ogrish. "My boss told me to."

"And that's it? You don't ask any questions?"

His expression didn't change. "No. Why would I?"

"What if your boss told you to kill me?"

He looked at her coolly. "I'm sure you'd be too smart to give him a reason to do that." He turned and walked out with Romano. To kill a man.

Zoey went into the bathroom and stepped into the tiny shower stall, blasting icy cold water all over her body. It didn't help.

She got dressed, reheated the rest of the coffee in the microwave, and berated herself for her weakness. One lap of Dominic's tongue and she'd been ready to abandon all of her principles and make the beast with two backs with … a real son of a beast. What the hell was wrong with her?

Her gloomy thoughts were interrupted by a sharp rapping on the door.

"Depends," she yelled. "Who is it?" Who even knew she was here? Right around now, that smell ability of Dominic's would come in handy.

The door rattled as someone messed with the lock. She leapt to her feet as the door swung open and Cin, Lorenzo, and Heath strolled in.

"Did you have to pick the lock?" Zoey said, annoyed. "You could have just said who you were and I'd have let you in!"

Cin shrugged. "Gotta keep my skills sharp."

Zoey turned her attention to Lorenzo. "Does your mom know you're here?"

"Will you can it with questions about my mom?" Lorenzo snapped. He never used to snap. Zoey looked at him steadily until he dropped his gaze. "Sorry."

"Call your mother and tell her where you are. Or leave."

"She'll yell at me!" He snuck a furtive glance at Cin, who looked faintly contemptuous.

Zoey had no sympathy. "You've earned it."

Grumbling, he grabbed his phone and headed into the hallway.

"Is lunch ready? Real roast beef!" Cin said, her eyes shining. "I'm drooling!"

"What?"

Cin looked puzzled. "The note you sent me? By gryphon messenger?"

Zoey shook her head in confusion. "I didn't send you a note."

"No roast beef?" Cin's shoulders slumped and she looked disappointed. "Man, I haven't had roast beef in like a year. My mom used to … never mind." Tears glittered in her eyes, and she blinked them away angrily. Zoey could see it wasn't the roast beef Cin was missing.

Like most of the homeless kids in Zoey's neighborhoods, Cin had been abandoned by her family when they found out she was a magic-blood. They still lived somewhere back east, but Cin didn't talk about them much.

Zoey glanced at the mini fridge in the kitchen. She suddenly noticed there was a bowl of fresh fruit sitting on top. It hadn't been there when she'd headed out in the morning. How had she missed that? Because she'd been too busy melting into a puddle of lust.

"Hold on," she said. She went over and yanked open the fridge door. It was full to the brim with sandwiches and cannolis and pots of tiramisu.

"Oh my God," Cin said reverently. "Come to mama."

"All that food," Heath said, his eyes big as saucers. "I'm going to have thirds and fourths."

Lorenzo came back in the room with a scowl that said his mother had chewed him out, but his face lit up when he saw Cin smiling.

The kids descended on the food like a pack of starving locusts. Zoey, who was famished after biking around town all morning, joined them. The roast beef was tender, the mayo was tangy, and the desserts were sweet, fluffy perfection.

They stuffed themselves until they were ready to burst, the kids sitting cross-legged on the floor because there weren't enough chairs.

Zoey felt guilty. Deliciously full but guilty. This was food from the Moretti Pack. She was eating murder food. Extortion food.

It also disturbed her that Dominic knew where to find Cin and her friends. That was why he'd sent them the note and steered them to her crash pad, she realized. Typical mobster—he was sending a message.

It was the kind of thing the Moretti Pack was known for. They sent gift baskets to merchants who fell behind on their payments, and they made sure to deliver it not to the stores but to the homes of the shop owners, parents, siblings, or mistresses.

If the merchants didn't catch up in a hurry, they'd disappear. They'd reappear in pieces piled up in front of their shop.

Today's food donation could be taken as a generous gesture, but it was also a veiled threat. *I know where your friends live.*

Dammit.

"You got the message from the gryphon delivery service?" Zoey quirked a brow at Cin.

"Yep," she replied cheerfully. "We were hanging outside the squat and the gryphon flew right over us and dropped it off."

"The person who sent you that gryphon … he's someone to be avoided. He was sending you the message to get to me. To let me know he knows where you live."

Cin and her friends exchanged uneasy glances.

"I know you move around pretty often. I hate to ask, but I think it's time to relocate. Could you possibly stay on the east side?"

The two packs stayed out of each other's territory. If Cin and her friends crashed in the Bianchi Pack territory, Dominic couldn't get to them.

The Bianchis wouldn't object or even notice. The sad advantage of being street urchins was, neither side cared what the kids did or where they slept. They didn't have jobs or own businesses, so it was pointless demanding protection money from them.

There were empty buildings scattered throughout the poorer districts; it wouldn't be hard for them to find a place to hide out.

"I guess we could," Cin shrugged.

"You need me to take care of this jerk for you?" Lorenzo puffed out his narrow chest.

Zoey forced herself not to laugh. "No, I'm afraid this is something I need to address on my own."

"All right. If you change your mind, just say the word." Lorenzo did his best to look fierce, and Zoey nodded appreciatively.

Cin shrugged. "We can stay at the old warehouse on 117th and Lombard."

Zoey nodded. "Yes, do that. And take all the leftover food."

"Seriously?" Cin squealed. "Best day ever!"

Zoey watched them enthusiastically filling up their backpacks, feeling a tightening frustration that a day with a full stomach was the best day ever for Cin.

CHAPTER SEVEN

"Well, hell." Giuliana rested her hands on her narrow hips and stared at the "Closed for Business" sign on the door of Carlito's Custom Wards. "Another one? My uncle's not going to be happy."

"You think?" Dominic growled.

Dominic, Romano and Giuliana were picking up protection money from the businesses in the mid-western section of Encantado. Always in cash; harder to trace that way. They were in a trendy shopping center called The Enchanted Circle, where mages sold items that catered to humans.

"Why would he close his business?" Romano asked, his thick brows drawing together. "He was the most popular ward-maker in the city."

"Exactly." Dominic shook his head. "Everything was fine last week. There was a line out the door, just like always."

The wards themselves were just small tiles of wood or clay with various runes carved into them and a hole at the top so they could be nailed next to doorways or windows with copper nails. What made them effective was the power imbued in them by mages.

Carlito was an exquisite artist. His wards had been featured in home decorating magazines. There was a waiting list to buy his more elaborate pieces; he took commissions from the city's elite.

Dominic pulled out his spell phone, scrolled through the phone numbers, and found Carlito's home number. When he called, he got the message it was disconnected.

He glanced up at Romano and Giuliana and shook his head. "I'll have someone swing by his house, but I'd bet my left paw he's already left town and we'll find nothing but dust bunnies."

"Carlito was dating a morning T.V. show host," Giuliana was always up to date with gossip. "She was on the air this morning, so she's still here. If he really has done a runner, like all those other business owners, that means he left behind his hot girlfriend, dumped a business that was making him a fortune, and paid a year's salary for the right to move to another portal city where he'd have to start over from scratch. Why?"

Why indeed? Dominic had tried to reach out to three other business owners, but he had no authority over them once they'd left Encantado, and they'd refused to speak to him.

"He had to have been running scared," Romano mused.

"But he could have come to us if anything, or anyone, had threatened him." Dominic ran his fingers through his hair, exasperated. "That's the whole point of protection money. Last year, when his shop was vandalized, he came to us, so it's not like he's been afraid to reach out."

Did these business owners know something he didn't? Was there some kind of attack coming? He was sure he'd have heard some underground chatter if that were the case.

Romano and Giuliana looked at him, waiting for orders.

"Go ask the lady at Charming if she knows anything," Dominic ordered. "Then meet us at the pastry shop."

Romano obediently trotted off to the little charm shop next door to Carlito's shuttered store.

Dominic and Giuliana went to the pastry shop on the other side of Carlito's former shop. The owner swore up and down she had no idea why Carlito had pulled a disappearing act. Dominic fetched two ice coffees while Giuliana settled down at a table and pulled out a magazine from her over-sized purse.

As he walked across the store, he felt the gazes of women as they stared with the usual mixture of fear and fascination.

He ignored them all. There was only one woman whose attention he wanted, and she was treating him like he had a communicable disease.

She'd come around though. Not like she had a choice.

He grimaced at the thought. No, he didn't want it to be like that. Some mafia shifter packs allowed their made men the "privilege" of snatching up any woman who caught their eye, whether she liked it or not.

Even if Arturo allowed it, which he wouldn't, Dominic would never force a woman.

Zoey had always liked Dominic—he knew that. He'd smelled the attraction on her the first time they met. He'd caught her sneaking glances at him when she thought he wasn't looking.

But she was stubborn and strong-willed and not familiar with shifter customs. He loved her strength and her pride, except when it stood in the way of her realizing they were meant for each other.

He needed to figure out a way to court her, which meant he'd have to ask an actual woman for advice.

And the only one he was on a semi-friendly basis was … ugh.

Dominic settled into the too-small chair facing Giuliana and shoved an iced coffee at her. She grabbed it and took a sip, still reading her magazine.

"Hey, brat, I have a favor to ask of you."

"What's in it for me?"

"I won't tell your uncle you never went to the mall yesterday like you said you did."

Giuliana set her magazine on her lap and flashed him a suspicious glower. "How did you … I mean, what are you talking about?"

"Please." Dominic gave her a scornful look. "I have eyes and ears everywhere."

She stamped her foot like a kindergartener being sent to take a nap. "I can go where I want. I'm twenty! I'm not a baby!"

Dominic refrained from telling her she sounded exactly like a baby when she pouted like that. He needed her advice. He might not have been the savviest when it came to women, but he knew better than to insult a tantruming she-shifter before asking for her help. Doing so would get him nothing but a set of bleeding scratches so deep they reached his internal organs. He'd been there, done that—it had taken hours to heal.

Glancing around to make sure nobody was listening, he cleared his throat and spoke in a lowered voice. "How do I romance a woman? What do women like?"

Giuliana scrunched up her nose in distaste.

"You've banged like a million bimbos. Were they not satisfied? Nobody's coming back for seconds?"

"I have had brief encounters in the past, and the women were very clear it was a one-time thing. That's not what I'm talking about."

"Who are you romancing? That chick from the slums?" She curled her lip in disdain.

Giuliana was really getting under his fur today. "Snobbery is beneath you. And yes. Since she's not shifter, I can't expect her to come trotting along with me when the time comes, not unless I take the time to do some wooing."

She lifted her skinny shoulders in a sullen shrug. "Then pick someone else."

Dominic gave her a sidelong glance. He hoped she didn't mean "pick me." He had assumed she didn't care who she mated with as long as it got her out from under her uncle's oppressive paw, but now he wasn't so sure. Ever since he'd mate-bitten Zoey, Giuliana seemed even crankier than usual.

"You know that's not how it works," he said. "Moon-bite. You were there."

She snorted and picked up her magazine again. "Fine. Take her out to dinner."

"That's all that you've got? Sorry I asked."

"If she doesn't appreciate what she has, she doesn't deserve you." Giuliana flipped a page and made a big show of ignoring him.

Dominic, annoyed and more than a little concerned, drained half his coffee and set it on the table. Since when did Giuliana give a damn about who he mated with? He'd dated women over the years, and she'd never seemed to care. Maybe she was upset because this was permanent? Damn, he hoped not. He liked Giuliana a lot as a person and would hate to hurt her. His life had enough complications right now.

Romano strolled over to the table with a scowl on his face that said trouble.

"The shop owner says she doesn't know anything. And I feel like I was being watched when I walked back here," he said to Dominic in a low voice. "My wolf's going crazy. I think it's someone in Greenwald Park."

CHAPTER *Eight*

Dominic glanced out the shop's big picture window. Greenwald Park was right across the main thoroughfare, a big park that ran east to west through the city center. He didn't see anything, but any enemy worth his salt would be hiding.

"Take Giuliana back home, I'll go check it out," he said.

Giuliana made a face. "If you're injured, I should be standing by so I can heal your dumb ass."

"You know what your uncle would say."

Dominic ignored her muttered curses. Giuliana's wolf was a large, vicious bitch who loved a good scrap, but her uncle treated her like a fragile china teacup. She'd tolerated it in her teens, but as she got older, she was growing increasingly frustrated. Dominic had heard Giuliana looked a great deal like Arturo's late daughter—the one he hadn't been able to save.

That was unfortunate for her. Arturo would probably never lighten up. He'd send the rest of his pack into the jaws of hell if necessary, but when it came to his niece, he just couldn't help himself.

As she stomped out with Romano hovering protectively over her, Dominic stopped at the counter to grab a roast beef sandwich. He was ninety-eight percent certain he was about to kick some ass, and he preferred not to do it hungry.

As he crossed the street, the hair on the back of his neck stood on end. Yep, he was being watched. Scanning the trees and hedges, the benches, and the people strolling by, he quickly took a path that led into the park.

Nothing looked out of place yet. A day-walker vampire and his thrall huddled under a tree as the vamp sucked on the girl's wrist. Her head was thrown back, eyes rolling in ecstasy. A group of college kids were playing hacky sack in a clearing. A young human nanny tried to pass him as she pushed a stroller down the path that led deeper into the park.

He shook his head at her. "Go back. Trouble," he said in a low voice, putting a hint of snarl in it to make sure she got the message.

Her eyes widened in fear, and she quickly wheeled the stroller around and jogged back toward the street.

The scent of an unfamiliar wolf drifted his way, and he headed toward it.

He kept eating as he walked. There wasn't a single wolf in the entire city of Encantado who worried him enough to make him put his sandwich down. And his wolf was snarling and howling now, clawing to be set free. To fight. To kill.

Apparently, the universe was willing to throw him a bone today because moments later, a wolf exploded from the bushes. The gray wolf was enormous, as were all warrior-class wolf shifters. Its eyes glowed yellow with fury as ropes of saliva dribbled from its black lips. It blocked his path, tail lashing. Dominic shoved the last of his sandwich into his mouth and brushed his hands off on his shirt, his bored expression unchanging.

The wolf stared at him blankly as if confused. It was likely more used to the sight of grown men running, screaming, and crying.

Angrily, it pulled back its lips and let out a low, rumbling growl that vibrated up from its chest.

"I'm going to give you a freebie," Dominic said, grinning fiercely. "Roll over and expose your belly, and I'll just maim you, not kill you. You can live another day as a member of the world's lamest pack."

The wolf threw back its head and howled in rage—the last howl of its life. It crouched low and then leapt, aiming for Dominic's throat. Dominic shifted in a blur of motion; nobody but Arturo could shift as quickly as he did. Twenty seconds later, the wolf was bleeding out at his feet, its throat ripped open and spinal column nearly severed.

Damn. What a thoroughly unsatisfying fight. He'd really been hoping they could go at least a couple rounds.

Dominic shook himself and forced his angry wolf back inside the cage of his humanity, his fur melting into smooth skin, tail shrinking into his spine, and fangs sinking back into his gums.

Dominic's clothes had fallen off when he shifted. A slender young woman in a business suit caught his eye and let her eyes rove over him before arching her eyebrows in invitation. He curled his lip and growled at her, letting fur ripple over his face. She stifled a shriek and hurried off. Good. The only woman who should be admiring his naked body was Zoey.

He dressed quickly, scowling down at the dead wolf which had melted back into its human form.

His phone rang, with the tone indicating it was Arturo. He snatched it from his jacket pocket.

"Let me guess," Dominic nudged the dead wolf with the toe of his boot, "the mage's board ruled in the Bianchi Pack's favor?"

"Close. The mage's board has decided to abstain," Arturo said. "They feel the law is unclear in this case, so they're not weighing in on either side."

Dominic felt a snap of anger. He hadn't expected that at all. "The law is clearly on our side. Can we appeal to the National Council?"

"It won't help. A full-out war between packs benefits the mages. Both of our packs are getting too powerful, and a battle royale would thin our ranks and possibly eliminate one of our packs altogether," Arturo replied. "This was always going to happen. Primo's never been happy sharing."

"Well, that explains why one of their soldiers is taking a dirt nap right now," Dominic mused. "He tried to jump me about sixty seconds ago."

"Huh. That was fast," Arturo said. "The ruling came down mere minutes ago. It's almost like he was lying in wait, just in case the ruling favored them. He's in our territory? Where are you?"

"Greenwald Park. It was Jimmy. He came at me from behind a bush. Primo was strategic about it, I'll give him that. You know about the rumors Jimmy was angling for Primo's position? And then Primo sent him to kill me. Whatever the results, it would have been a win for Primo." If Jimmy failed, Primo had let someone else kill one of his enemies. If he had succeeded, he would have made the Moretti Pack look weak, and he also would have taken out one of Arturo's strongest warriors.

"Wait a minute." Arturo's voice suddenly went sharp. "Isn't Giuliana with you right now? Oh, never mind, I see she's heading back to my office."

"Romano is with her; she's fine. And they wouldn't mess with a non-combatant female unless they want every shifter pack in the country to declare war on them," Dominic said. "Wait ... do you have a tracker on your niece?"

Silence.

"So something in her phone or on her clothing," Dominic mused. "Nah, she'd suspect the phone. If she wanted to sneak out, she'd leave it behind. Maybe something on a piece of jewelry?"

There was a long pause.

"Don't tell her." Arturo's voice sounded surprisingly mild.

"Of course not, sir."

Giuliana would tantrum and throw things at her uncle, or she'd try to run away. If she ran, Arturo would catch her and lock her up for a month and Giuliana would make everyone's life hell.

Arturo's voice turned brisk and business-like. "Right. Attack on a pack member. We'll have to answer." By which he meant, kill someone from the Bianchi Pack or blow up something they owned. "Meet me at my office in forty-five minutes. Don't bother fetching Giuliana. I'll text her."

Dominic headed straight for the Arena. Giuliana was already there, with Otto and Arturo, sitting in chairs arranged in front of Arturo's desk. They were skipping the socializing today; Arturo was pissed. His ears had gone pointy and furry, and he didn't even bother smoothing them out.

"Are you all right?" Giuliana asked Dominic with genuine concern. "You should have let me stay. I could have—"

"You could have stayed out of it or I'd have grounded you until you were dead," Arturo snapped.

"You can't treat me like I'm a damned pup," she muttered rebelliously.

Arturo twisted to the side to fix her with his icy gaze. "What was that?"

"Nothing." She inclined her head to the left, exposing her throat in a show of submission.

"Yes, that's what I thought you said. Nothing." Then he addressed Dominic – making a big show of ignoring his niece. "We're going to hijack one of their armored trucks tomorrow morning," Arturo said. "Hit those bastards where it hurts—in the wallet."

Dominic nodded. "I'm going to suggest we take his men prisoner rather than kill them. That way we—"

"Bullshit!" Ottavio barked, interrupting him.

"Let him finish," Arturo ordered.

Dominic continued as if Ottavio hadn't said a word. "We actually make ourselves look better this way. We're not just fighting the Bianchis, we're fighting a war of perception. Right now, the Bianchis are presenting themselves as the aggrieved party. If we choose not to kill, it shows the Council of Mages we're exercising restraint. We're not the troublemakers. If we take the men hostage and hold them for ransom, that's double humiliation for the Bianchis."

Zoey would approve of the less violent option.

He didn't know why thoughts of her were popping into his head at a time like this, but he remembered the look on her face when he told her he had to go kill a man. He hadn't liked the way it made him feel.

"Can I suggest another tactic?" Ottavio vibrated with anger, his voice a raspy growl.

"No." Arturo dismissed him and turned away. "You will be in charge of this, Dominic."

"Sir?" Ottavio struggled to keep the anger from his voice, but he couldn't hide his claws as they shot from his fingertips.

"This situation calls for diplomacy," Arturo said curtly. "You tend to kill first and ask questions afterward."

"But Ott, how else would we do it?" Carlo sounded confused. Ouch," he added as his brother punched him in the arm.

"Shut it, Carlo," Ottavio said with a glower.

CHAPTER *Nine*

The community center was crowded with angry residents and business owners. Even with the windows and doors shut, the sour smell of garbage permeated the air. Jordan sat in the front row in his flashy suit and nice shoes.

Zoey, Danielle, Stewart, Lorenzo, and Andrea stood at the podium as Zoey made her pitch.

The group had decided to let Zoey do the talking about her plan for the community gardens because her enthusiasm was contagious. Danielle, who had taken the night off from work, stood next to her and drank coffee with her usual sour expression.

"We'll have the greenest space in all of Encantado! And we can use the fruit and vegetables we grow to set up a free community kitchen!" Zoey finished. That had been her favorite part.

Apparently, the audience didn't agree. They just stared at the group with expressions of horror on their faces.

"Gee, tough crowd," Zoey murmured to Danielle, taken aback.

"What a bunch of buttwipes," Danielle said indignantly. "We worked hard on this plan. Well, you and Stewart and Andrea worked hard on this plan and I offered moral support. I whined less than usual."

"Yes, you did." Zoey bobbed her head in agreement.

Andrea had kept Danielle's mouth stuffed with apple dumplings, and as long as Danielle was chewing, she wasn't bitching.

Zoey cleared her throat and pasted a big smile on her face. "If we can help out the homeless community here, there will be less crime, which benefits all of us!" she said into the microphone, her voice bouncing off the walls.

Not a word. Everyone just stared in her direction in frozen dismay.

"Oh. It's not you," Danielle said in a low voice. She flicked a nervous glance at Zoey. "I think there's actually something behind us."

Zoey stood perfectly still, suddenly aware of every beat of her heart. In Encantado, "something behind us" could be ... very scary. She just prayed it wasn't a ghoul. She didn't want to spend her final hours in a killing rage ripping her friends' flesh from their bones with her teeth. They probably didn't want that either.

Then again, she'd have smelled a ghoul. From what she'd heard, they reeked enough that even garbage wouldn't disguise their odor.

The two women turned around very slowly.

Ottavio and Carlo had just walked in the room through the back door and were standing behind them.

Lorenzo's face lit up as he looked at them admiringly. "The Moretti Pack? Wow!" His mother smacked him on the arm.

The room was completely silent.

Danielle went pale and her coffee cup slipped from her fingers.

Ottavio opened his mouth to speak, but Dominic and Romano burst through a side door, and his mouth snapped shut again. From the look on Ottavio's face, he hadn't been expecting them and wasn't happy to see them. Carlo just stood there, glowering at the room with dull menace.

Ottavio stormed over and started talking to Dominic and Romano in low, angry tones. While the men argued, the audience members jumped to their feet and ran for the doors as if their butts were on fire.

Jordan stood frozen in place, with an uncertain look on his face, his eyes darting between Dominic and Ottavio.

Ottavio crossed the room swiftly and stopped in front of Jordan, whose eyes widened in terror. "I understand you have been collecting fees but not paying the garbage collection company," he said in a loud voice, although there was hardly anyone left in the room to hear him.

"But I—" Jordan started to protest.

Ottavio quickly shifted and ripped out Jordan's throat with his teeth. A fountain of scarlet jetted up from Jordan's throat, and he staggered backward and crumpled into a heap.

Andrea went pale and grabbed Lorenzo's arm and dragged him off as he protested and tried to pull away from her.

Stewart hurried after them, taking care to put his body between them and Ottavio.

Danielle bolted for the nearest doorway. She stopped to look for Zoey, who was standing on the stage, too stunned to move.

"Zoey, come *on*!" she screeched, and then ran for it.

Ottavio's enormous gray wolf licked blood from his lips, and Zoey's stomach lurched. He shifted back into human form and bent down to pick up his clothing from the floor.

After he'd hastily dressed, he scowled at Dominic. "You didn't need to come here. I had it handled."

"Since it involves my mate, yes, I did need to come. And you shouldn't have tried to keep me out of it." Dominic's voice held an edge of steel.

"I don't report to you," Ottavio growled. "I serve only Arturo. You'd do well to remember that." Ottavio left without a backward glance with Carlo trailing behind him.

Dominic walked over to the podium and helped Zoey climb down. "You all right?"

She struggled to find her voice. "A little shaken."

"Jordan was pocketing the money. We only found out today," he said, grimacing. "He told us the neighborhood had gone on strike because they thought our fees were too high. We'll make sure all this garbage is cleaned up by end of day tomorrow. And next time there's a problem like this, you'll contact me immediately."

Zoey swayed on her feet and struggled not to barf. Jordan had been a horrible human being, but seeing him killed right in front of her had snatched the breath from her body. She backed away from Dominic.

"Is that an order?"

He didn't pursue her, so she stopped moving. "That is a request," he said calmly. "Your friends live here, right? If this neighborhood has issues, you'd want them taken care of, wouldn't you? So if you need help, ask me."

She glanced at Jordan's body. She couldn't stand here having a conversation with a dead body ten feet away from her and the smell of blood clotting her nostrils. She turned and hurried out the back door.

Dominic was right on her heels. He moved to block her as she hurried down the steps. "Where do you think you're going?" he snapped. "I was talking to you." Romano trailed behind him but stood back, giving them space.

"I just saw a man killed right in front of me! Excuse me if I can't make casual conversation next to a corpse!" She burst into tears.

"Oh," he said, sounding chastened. "I'm sorry. Really sorry." He gathered her in his arms, and her knees went wobbly as she leaned into him.

"I apologize," he said gently, stroking her back. "I've lived this lifestyle so long, death just doesn't have much impact on me."

"Well, maybe it should," she said, sniffling hard.

"Yes," he said, his voice surprisingly wistful. "Maybe it should."

Zoey slumped against him and rested her head against his shoulders, letting him hold her up. The feeling of his fingers trailing down her back was soothing, and when she closed her eyes, she felt like the rest of the world had faded away and they were in their own little bubble, just the two of them.

She'd never let herself be weak like this and hadn't ever leaned on anyone else for strength. It felt so good, she let a minute or two drag by. Finally, she stepped back. Dominic released her reluctantly, his muscular arms dropping back to his side.

She heaved a sigh, missing his warmth and his scent of piney cologne and animal musk. She couldn't let this happen again; it would be too easy to get addicted to a man like Dominic.

"You should have kissed her!" Romano called out helpfully. "Too late now."

Dominic shot a furious glance at him. "I. Will. End. You."

Romano smiled back, looking very unafraid.

Dominic managed a rueful smile at Zoey. "Ignore him. He was dropped on his head a lot as a pup. Now, where were we?"

"All right," Zoey said, hugging herself. "You had no idea our payments weren't going where they're supposed to?"

"Of course not." Dominic looked offended. "I don't know how the hell Jordan thought he could get away with this."

"Well, he wasn't the brightest bulb on the tree."

Zoey tried to wrap her head around what he'd just told her. She had been livid at the thought of the Moretti Pack ripping off poor communities and leaving them to live in filth with no recourse. If that wasn't true, did it change how she felt about Dominic?

He was still violent and aggressive and a killer, but he was also capable of surprising tenderness and protectiveness.

"It will never happen again," Dominic told her. "I'll be visiting the head of the garbage company first thing tomorrow. I understand a number of people complained to him and told him they'd paid their fees. He should have reported that to us."

Alarm flashed through her. "You're not going to kill him, are you?"

He looked puzzled. "Why wouldn't I?"

"Why wouldn't you just *end someone's life?*" Zoey felt a surge of frustration. There was a part of her that wanted to like Dominic, to let him in and trust him, but when he treated murder as if it were some casual chore, he made it hard. "Because it's wrong. Because we have police and a court system to deal with things like fraud. I mean, for that matter, why even bother? The people in power here take whatever they can get away with, and the only reason you guys stepped in was because it was getting so bad here, it was impossible to pretend you didn't know what was happening."

"Is that how you see things?" Dominic replied crisply.

She gestured around her at the piles of stinking trash heaped around overflowing garbage cans up and down the street. "That's how it is, Dominic."

His brow creased. "That's not how Arturo runs things, and it will not happen again. I'm going to personally visit each of our neighborhood liaisons and let them know if they ever try to pull what Jordan did, they'll find out the true meaning of the word 'pain.'"

"None of this would have happened if things ran like they did outside of the portal cities," she said with an accusing scowl. "What gives you the right to collect protection money in the first place? We pay taxes and have to pay you too?"

He raised his eyebrows questioningly. "Do the police give you protection, Zoey?"

She winced. "Well, not always, but in fairness, the police force can't really handle magical threats all by themselves, even with their mage and shifter divisions. They're overwhelmed. Their departments are, I think, ninety percent human, according to what I read in The Encantado Telegraph. Entire neighborhoods are no-go zones. There's only so much they can do."

"Exactly. We provide a service. We charge people for that service. If you visit any other neighborhood in our territory, you'll see we keep the promises we make. What we charge is like a tax. Unlike the government agencies, though, we have the magical mojo to back it up." He stared into her eyes, his gaze holding hers captive. The intensity in his voice made her feel like he really, really cared what she thought.

"If you say so." Zoey flicked another glance at the garbage and shoved her hands in the pockets of her jeans. Down the block, she saw Danielle watching her from behind a telephone pole.

She waved her hand at Danielle to let her know everything was okay. Danielle gave her a puzzled look, glancing from Dominic to her, and then turned and headed back to their apartment.

"You'll see I'm telling the truth when the garbage is gone tomorrow," Dominic said. "I was going to take you out to dinner, but I understand you probably don't have much of an appetite now. I'll walk you home instead."

"Would there be any point in arguing?"

He grinned at her. "Please do. I find it so entertaining."

She shot him a sidelong look of defiance. "I greatly look forward to being walked home by you. Thank you so much for that chivalrous gesture."

"Spoilsport." He flashed her a charming grin.

Before she could stop herself, Zoey replied with a smile. She quickly rearranged her facial features into an indifferent mask, but it was too late—he looked entirely too smug and self-satisfied.

They walked back to her apartment without another word. Halfway there, he slid his arm around her shoulders, and it felt natural to Zoey. He was so big and warm, and she found herself letting him pull her up against him so her hip pressed against his thigh. As they walked, they fell into a rhythm somehow, his stride matching hers even though he was easily a foot taller than her.

Warmth rolled over her, along with a pulsing arousal.

Is he proportionally big all over?

She choked down a mortified laugh at the thought, and he gave her a bemused glance but didn't say anything. They paused in front of the doorway to her apartment building. The protection wards glowed, and the door clicked open.

Romano stood half a block away from them, pretending not to watch. She thought Dominic would insist on coming in, but instead, he slid a finger under her chin and tipped her head back to give her a soft, feather-light kiss that sent a jolt of desire rushing through her.

Zoey swallowed a moan of frustration and hurried into her apartment when he walked away. She was dying to ask him why he wasn't just grabbing her and dragging her home with him if he was so sure she was meant to be his. But she didn't because she was afraid he might take her up on it. And she was even more afraid she wouldn't have the strength to say no.

CHAPTER TEN

In District 17, there was rarely such a thing as a good surprise.

Surprises usually were quickly followed by large crowds of people running and screaming, the sounds of explosions, and the odor of things catching on fire.

That's why Zoey wasn't thrilled to see a note slipped under her door.

> I've got a surprise for you! Come to 133rd Street and Sierra Avenue today at noon.

It was signed "Your Mate," with a pawprint inked next to the words.

She pondered the note for a good half hour, but finally, curiosity got the best of her. Zoey tried to wake up Danielle, but she flat-out refused because she had worked the overnight shift. Andrea was on deadline making a logo for a witch's coven, Stewart was nowhere to be found, and Lorenzo was in a mood, so Zoey went by herself.

What could possibly be worth seeing at a vacant lot the size of a city block?

But it was no longer vacant.

There was a giant canvas tent in the middle of the lot, with a curious crowd milling outside. As Zoey made her way through the crowd, she saw a sign on the front of the tent: "District 17 Community Garden, Grand Opening Tomorrow."

She walked up to the tent flap, and it was jerked aside. Dominic loomed over her, casting a long shadow in the bright sunshine. He wore a navy-blue suit, making her feel very underdressed in her t-shirt and distressed denim jeans.

He looked extremely pleased with himself as he stepped aside and gestured at her to enter.

There were some cries of "How come she gets to go in and we don't?" from the crowd. Dominic quickly silenced them with a rumbling growl and yanked the tent flap shut behind him.

Inside was a small miracle.

Raised garden beds in galvanized steel bins, easily a hundred of them, were lined up in neat rows. They were filled with rich, dark, fragrant earth. A dozen compost bins were installed along the right side of the tent. Water pipes snaked along the ground and climbed the garden beds.

There were even picnic tables with benches and umbrellas scattered throughout the lot.

"This is amazing," Zoey said in wonder as she strode past the raised beds with Dominic at her side.

She trailed her finger along the edge of one of the beds. The earth quivered, and she faintly sensed the seedlings underneath. "We can pull together lists of volunteers to water and weed the plants, and I can find some more garden witches to hang out here with me a few times a week so the plants will be nice and healthy. We can get the homeless kids involved, maybe give each of them their own garden bed to tend so they feel invested …" She stopped and looked at Dominic and flashed him a huge, grateful smile. "Thank you."

Dominic bowed at the waist. "It's not half bad, if I do say so myself," he said with transparently false modesty. "This is the Moretti Pack's way of making up for the garbage issue."

He gestured at one of the picnic tables at the far end of the garden, and Zoey realized there was a large wicker picnic basket on the table.

"You're in luck," she said.

The picnic basket was filled with sandwiches wrapped in wax paper, luscious ripe apples and pears and grapes, potato salad, and bottles of lemonade.

There were two china plates already set out for them, along with napkins and silverware. He'd thought of everything.

He sat across from her, smiling. She bit into a sandwich and nodded in appreciation.

"Kalinda made this, didn't she?"

"Yeah, I figured she'd know what you'd like. How could you tell?"

Zoey finished chewing, almost groaning in pleasure. "I recognize the dressing. She puts something special in it. She won't tell me what it is though."

"I could make her talk," Dominic said, and then he saw her appalled look. "Kidding?"

"Were you?"

"Mostly." He looked disgruntled. "I mean, of course, I'm capable of making anyone talk, but I would never do such a thing. For a sandwich recipe. If it was your friend." He smiled at her. "She asked how you were doing and said she hoped I was treating you well. I swear it sounded like there was a hint of a threat there. She's got some brass ones."

Zoey nearly choked on her sandwich as she laughed at the mental image he'd just conjured up. "I've been in changing rooms with her, and I'm fairly sure she does not possess what you just described. But yes, she is very protective of the girls who work for her. In her own special, stressed-out, taking-the-weight-of-the-world-on-her-shoulders way."

When she finished her sandwich, Zoey reached for a slice of cake.

"So? You approve?" Dominic reached for his third sandwich. Damn, that wolf's metabolism didn't quit.

"I more than approve. I love." She wondered if she could get away with asking for a community center with a basketball court but decided not to push her luck. For now.

"If you like this, wait until you see the pack compound."

He was provoking her now, implying she was going to actually be visiting the pack compound any time soon, but she wasn't going to take the bait.

"I'm sure it's amazing." Zoey smiled politely as she reached for a bottle of lemonade.

"You'll love it."

He just couldn't let it go, could he?

After they finished eating, Dominic quickly put their plates and empty bottles back into the picnic basket and stood.

"I want to show you something." He walked over to the raised bed nearest the picnic table. There were rows of tiny little leaflets poking through the rich, dark loam. "That was nothing but dirt when we sat down. You see what you've done? That is an amazing talent, and I don't think you appreciate how truly special you are. You nurture life."

"That's a nice way to look at it." Zoey sighed. "Honestly, it's hard to feel anything but resentment for my talent. It's strong enough to get me banished from my home, but not strong enough to be actually worth anything. I'm like a Level 2 on a good day."

"Your power is probably stronger than you know," Dominic said. "It's common for magic bloods to suppress their power if they grew up outside the portal cities. It's a survival instinct. But if you're trained to embrace your power, it has the potential to strengthen and expand." He gestured at her. "Come over here, and let's try something."

"Are you going to get fresh with me?"

His roguish grin was irresistible. "God, I hope so."

She walked over next to him and stood right up against the raised bed.

Dominic moved until he was almost touching her. She leaned into him, drawn by his musky scent and the heat that pumped from his body.

"Put your hands in the dirt and close your eyes." She gave him a suspicious look. "I promise not to try anything. At least not while your eyes are closed."

Zoey shoved her hands into the earth and immediately felt energy vibrating up through her fingers. She found herself instinctively clamping shut, tensing up, the way she had her entire life. Since she was young, she'd known she was cursed with the faintest trace of magic, but for the longest time, she had let herself believe if she ignored it, it would wither and die.

But Dominic was right. There was beauty in earth magic and helping things grow. Maybe it wasn't entirely a curse.

She closed her eyes, and her muscles went rigid.

"Your whole body is tensing. Just relax. Let the power of the earth flow through you."

She opened her eyes and looked up at him. "How do you know this stuff?"

"Because I've lived here for a long time, and because training for magic-bloods is similar to training for wolves that have just turned. Born wolves don't need training, but made wolves do. We have to get comfortable with our animal, we have to get in touch with it so we don't suppress it, and also so we don't let it burst out at inappropriate moments."

He fell silent. She stood there and willed herself to relax.

Loosen up, stupid muscles! Chill out, brain!

Not working.

"Telling myself to relax just makes me feel more tense. I'm sorry. I'm really not very good at this."

"Then don't try so hard. Think of something else. Picture something you love."

Zoey felt an odd tension in Dominic's body when he said that, even though they weren't touching. She sensed it on a deep, painful level.

"Did you lose something you loved, Dominic?" she asked softly.

"Someone. A long time ago. It's one reason I am so protective of you." She could hear the distant sadness in his voice. "And one reason I'm such an ass a lot of the time."

"If you ever want to talk about it, I'm here for you."

"I'm not ready yet." The gruffness was back in his voice.

At least he'd said "yet." Maybe someday he'd be willing to share a little more of himself.

She leaned into him and relaxed.

Zoey pictured her mother's face, her father, and her younger brothers and sister. She imagined them at a day on the beach, the sun beaming down on them, the gentle swishing sound of the ocean.

Her mother was watching her siblings like a hawk and shrieking at them when they paddled out too far. Her father was cooking on their portable grill and sneaking glances at his wife and kids when they thought he wasn't looking because he was supposed to be the chill one.

Gradually, Zoey's muscles started to relax. Then she felt the power of the earth flowing through her, and a surge of energy rushed up to her feet and out through her fingertips. She didn't have to open her eyes to know the plants in the bin were growing. She could feel the cells dividing and leaves unfurling. Waves of power rushed through her, and she started to feel dizzy. She clamped down on her power and shut it off, like turning a spigot.

She swayed where she stood, and Dominic had his arms around her waist, gently supporting her.

She looked down. All of the tomato plants in the bed, dozens of them, had grown several inches. She had never grown so many plants so quickly.

"Whoa. You did amazing." He guided her over to a bench, and she sank down, knees giving out. He sat next to her, silently resting his hand on her knee. It took a few minutes before the dizziness passed, but she didn't feel drained—she felt calm.

She looked him in the eye. There really was more to him than she had ever given him credit for.

"I want to get to know you," she blurted out. "I won't mate with a stranger."

He nodded. "All right, I'll make you a deal. For every kiss you give me, I will let you ask me one question."

Uh oh. *Danger, danger.*

When it came to Dominic, Zoey had certain self-control issues.

But he had information she needed, and this was the only way she would get it. And his lips were so soft, and so close …

She leaned in and brushed her lips against his. He gently cupped her chin with one hand and tangled his other hand in her hair, and she parted her lips. She could still faintly taste the sweet, tart lemonade from the picnic.

His tongue swirled around hers in a slow, sensual dance. She moved a little closer tilted her head back. Somehow, she was pressed up against him, her breasts nestling into his hard, muscled chest.

He'd removed his hand from her hair and wrapped his arm around her waist, crushing her into him. When had that happened? Overhead, she heard birds chirping, a chorus of music just for them. Far off in the distance, she heard the squawk of the phoenix.

Dominic stroked her face gently, and she savored his sweet taste and the feeling of the muscles bunching in his arm. Good God, if he kissed like that, what else could he do with that mouth? An image flashed through Zoey's mind of her sprawled out on her bed, with him between her legs, his tongue swirling and teasing and …

A honking car horn jerked her back to reality, and she pulled away. "Good Lord, did you get a PhD in kissing? Or is there a love potion in your Chapstick?" She was breathless.

"No, I didn't get a PhD in kissing, you just inspire me. And there is nothing in my Chapstick. Because I don't use it."

She shook her head, trying to clear it. "Wow."

His face was so close to hers, giving her a chance to study it intimately. It was really unfair for any man to be that handsome. He had a few little scars, which was not surprising given he was a shifter and worked in a profession where he got in a lot of fights. But the scars just enhanced his rugged good looks.

"Okay so my question is—"

"Hold on." Dominic held up his hand in a "stop" gesture. "You actually just asked two questions. You asked if I had a PhD in kissing, and if I put something in my Chapstick. Technically, you owe me another kiss, but I'm a generous guy so I'll allow two for the price of one."

"What?" Zoey shoved back from him on the bench, sliding as far away as she could get without falling off. "You are such a cheater!"

He smirked. "How did I cheat?"

"Well, you … But I … If you don't stop looking so smug, I'm going to pop you one. That's how."

Dominic shook his head. "You have many wonderful qualities, Zoey, but I would suggest you don't go to law school because your debate skills leave something to be desired." He leaned back in his seat, holding his muscular arms open wide. "The offer is still open. A kiss for a question."

She took a deep breath. Okay, she could do this. She was stronger than her libido. She'd show him this time. One kiss, ten seconds tops, and then she'd pull away and ask him her question.

Zoey moved close to him, and he circled his arm around her waist, pulling her to him. He still tasted so good, and his lips were pillow soft. She started counting down in her head, but then she lost track of the numbers and got confused. What came after five again? More kissing, that's what.

This time, she lifted her hands and stroked his face, enjoying the rasp of his stubble under her fingers.

He devoured her mouth with increasing fervor. She slid her hands along his broad chest and began undoing his top button. God, what an amazing body he must have. She wanted to run her hands over every inch of it, to kiss it, to taste …

Oh hell, it was happening again!

She pulled away from him and leaped to her feet with a shriek of frustration.

Dominic groaned in frustration. "Zoey!"

She ignored him and hurried from the tent, her cheeks flaming in embarrassment. What had just possessed her?

She pushed her way through the crowd and rushed back home. She was already in her apartment when she realized she hadn't even asked him her question.

Chapter Eleven

The wind had a crisp chill to it. Two hostile groups of wolf shifters stood a short distance apart from each other on a road in the rural area just north of Encantado city limits.

Primo Bianchi's dull black eyes fixed on Arturo as if he hoped to make him burst into flames with his gaze alone. Primo's men crowded around him, bristling with aggression and peeling their lips back to show their fangs.

Arturo didn't seem to notice they were there. He stood with Romano, Dominic, Ottavio, and Carlo, making idle conversation. His lack of response to the Bianchi Pack seemed to aggravate Primo even more, which was entirely the point.

There had been a ghoul attack nearby hours earlier. A man had been killed while he was mowing his lawn. His neighbor had called the police and sirens had alerted all of the residents to take shelter indoors. A police squadron had arrived and quickly killed two ghouls who were tearing at the door of a small ranch house.

The Council of Mages had ordered the two packs to temporarily set aside their feud. Both packs had been summoned there to send out their best scenters to find out where the ghouls had come from.

Benedict stood by the roadside, sipping hot tea from a cardboard cup and watching silently. If either pack attacked the other during the search, they would be punished.

The scenters and foot soldiers were searching the woods, following the ghouls' trail.

Where could they have come from? It didn't make any sense. There was only the one portal, and it was constantly guarded.

"What if it's a new larger portal?" Dominic mused. "A permanent one?"

"That wouldn't happen in our territory!" Ottavio growled. "We've got it under control!"

"Yeah, we've got it unner a troll!" Carlo echoed, always loyal to his brother. "Wait, there's a troll?"

Ottavio waved his hand at him, making a shushing motion. "Carlo, leave the talking to me."

Dominic snorted. Ottavio believed brute force was the answer to everything. He was an idiot. Sheer numbers and physical strength of their pack had no more to do with a portal opening than it had to do with a volcano erupting. They were forces of nature; they just happened.

"We have to consider all possibilities," Arturo said calmly.

"Of course, we do," Ottavio agreed instantly.

Dominic rolled his eyes. Ottavio was a dull echo for everything Arturo said. If the man ever had an original thought, it would die of loneliness.

Carlo looked at him in confusion. "That's not what you just said."

Ottavio was usually patient with his brother, but he'd clearly had enough today. He let out a snarl and bunched up his fist, but Arturo interrupted him.

"Stop," he said in an icy tone before flicking a glance at Primo. Primo glared back at them with fierce intensity. "Do you want him to see us as divided?"

"Of course not." Ottavio shifted his weight from one foot to another. "I just get antsy seeing them over there looking at us like that. It's not good for the pack, letting them treat us with disrespect."

"Matters will come to a head sooner rather than later." Arturo shrugged.

"Can't come soon enough for me." Ottavio flashed his fangs at the Bianchis and quickly retracted them.

Dominic strolled off to call one of the men he had watching Zoey. The answer he got made him growl. She was working her bike messenger job today and kept managing to shake his people and disappear for long stretches of time.

She was surprisingly good at dodging his men, better than she should have been. She was new to the city, and his men were pros, so how was she doing it?

It wasn't just that he was a control freak and antsy about the possibility of other men flirting with her. He also wanted to be able to keep her safe. She hadn't lived in Encantado that long, and she had such a naturally decent nature.

He wished there was something he could do about that.

What if she trusted the wrong person? What if she stopped to help someone with a flat tire and it turned out to be a trap? Or she went to give money to a panhandler and they stabbed her?

He shook his head impatiently, trying to clear his thoughts. What the hell was wrong with him? As a member of a mafia pack, he was accustomed to loss. People died, plain and simple. You accepted it, you moved on. No matter how strong he was, no matter what powers he had, Dominic couldn't be everywhere at once, watching everyone close to him all the time.

That was the way it was in portal cities. He'd learned that lesson a decade ago, and it had nearly destroyed him. Hell, in some ways it had—he'd never be the man he used to be.

Since then, he'd built a stone wall around his heart to protect it, and nobody had ever breached it. It wasn't like him to worry like this. Hell, Zoey wasn't even officially bonded to him, not until the next full moon.

But the thought of anything happening to her nearly made his fur burst from his skin.

He called his man again. "Did you find her yet?"

"In the last sixty seconds?" his guard squawked incredulously.

"Excuse you?" Dominic barked into the phone. "What the fuck did you just say to me?"

The guard took in a sharp breath. "I will find her and report back immediately."

"Yeah, that's what I thought you said." Dominic hung up and shoved the phone back into his pocket.

He needed to step up his game and show Zoey the benefits of being with him. Maybe he could find some suggestions on the internet? No, that was just embarrassing. If anyone ever saw "how to woo your reluctant mate" in his search history, he'd have to kill them. Or let himself get eaten by an ogre.

"Here comes someone. Oh, it's just Fabiana," Romano announced.

Fabiana was a scenter, so she'd been included in the search party. She came trotting out of the woods and walked toward the Moretti Pack instead of the Bianchis.

She shifted and stood naked before them, blinking her big brown eyes. Arching her back, she made a huge show of tossing her shiny black hair over her shoulder, looking right at Dominic as she did so.

"Romano, leave us." She flipped a slim hand in dismissal. "I need to speak to my future mate." Turning her attention to Dominic, she batted her eyes. "I've thought about it, and I'm willing to forgive you. You were drinking the night you bit her. It must have effected your wolf's judgement."

"Don't give orders to my men. And as for you, I'd rather mate with a ghoul," Dominic said coldly.

"You cannot seriously want to shackle yourself to that fat little nobody!" Fabiana's eyes blazed in anger.

Fur rippled over Dominic's face, and his claws shot from his fingertips. "Do not *ever* speak of my mate like that again!" he snarled.

She stepped back and burst into tears. "Don't hurt me!" she cried out loudly.

Fake-cringing, she raised her hands in front of her face. As if. She-shifters were vicious as hell when cornered. If he'd made a move to hurt her, she'd have shifted and gone straight for a vital organ. Probably the one between his legs.

Dammit. Fabiana had deliberately provoked him, and he'd fallen for it like an idiot.

Primo and Luigi came barreling toward them. The Moretti Pack members rushed to Dominic's side.

Benedict stood back and sipped his tea, watching the show with an expression of mild interest.

"You threaten my female?" Primo bellowed. "That is a new low, even for you!"

"You really are spoiling for a showdown, which we are happy to provide right here," Arturo drawled. "Your hearing is every bit as good as ours, and you know exactly what your female just did to provoke my *Capo*. What would you do if one of your females came up and barked orders at a made man like that?"

"Bite her face off!" Luigi snapped furiously.

Primo spun around and punched Luigi in the head so hard he fell to his knees. "You do not speak for me!" he growled.

Primo sent a wave of force so intense, they all felt it, and Luigi clawed at his throat, eyes wide and panicked.

Fabiana's gaze shuttled nervously back and forth between the Bianchis and the Morettis. She was one of those women who got through life manipulating men by either seducing them or stirring up trouble by flirting with mated men.

Dominic felt a faint burning discomfort, and Romano grimaced, but Primo's powers were nowhere near as strong as Arturo's.

Finally, Primo released Luigi, who fell to his hands and knees, his face purple. He gasped and wheezed, desperately sucking in air.

"Your questioning this makes no sense," Arturo said coldly. "Your parents' pairing was a moon-bite."

"My father was actually choosing a mate. He was not trying to get out of a legitimate mating contract by biting the first floozy who—" Primo suddenly turned red and clawed at his throat.

Arturo pumped out waves of power that made Dominic's head hurt. Everyone backed up quickly. Although Arturo was directing the power straight at Primo, it affected those around him.

Several of Primo's men hurried forward to try to help, and Arturo's power caught them up too. They gasped, their eyes bulging from their heads. The rest of Primo's men backed up warily.

Benedict hurried over. "Enough!" he bellowed. "I demand you release them! If you wish to kill Primo, issue a formal challenge and do it by the book."

"Very well." Arturo released all of them. They collapsed, faces purplish, wheezing and clawing at their throats.

When Primo could speak again, he turned to Benedict. "You saw what he did to us!" he croaked.

"I remain neutral." Benedict stepped back, a smirk curling his lips.

Fucking weasel.

Benedict and the rest of the mages would be delighted to stand back and watch the two packs fight to the death.

"Do you wish to meet me in the death arena?" Arturo demanded. "You can bring two of your strongest men with you; it won't help."

Primo stared at him with burning hatred. Arturo had just humiliated him. If Primo said yes, Arturo would kill him in the arena. If he didn't agree, he looked weak in front of everybody.

The moment stretched on and on. Primo shook with rage. Arturo had dismissed Primo completely as any kind of threat.

Boom. *Now* Arturo had just handed him the ultimate humiliation.

"Here they come," Romano called out and gestured at the woods. The scenters and the foot soldiers came trotting out, looking as glum as wolves could look. They shifted back to human form and walked up to the roadside, pulling on the clothing they'd left behind.

Arturo snapped his fingers at Ciro, his best scenter. "What did you find?" he said impatiently.

"The scent goes through the woods to a small dirt road and then vanishes," Ciro said, looking frustrated.

"Like they were let out of a car?" Arturo raised a brow.

"That's difficult for me to say. The road has a lot of car smells, some fresher than others." Ciro frowned. "I'm sorry, boss, we didn't find any sign of a lesser portal, and we have no idea where they could have come from." The other shifters nodded.

Primo gestured impatiently at his lead scenter, a wolf named Pasquale.

"We found the same thing." He made a face as if agreeing with the Moretti Pack's scenters left a sour taste in his mouth.

"So both of you failed," Benedict said irritably. He scowled at Primo. "Your pack leaves first. The Moretti Pack will wait twenty minutes. You both will return to your respective territories before hostilities are permitted to commence." He headed to his car and drove off.

Arturo waited until the Bianchi Pack left before gesturing at his men. "Wait for me in the cars. You too," he added to Romano, who glanced briefly at Dominic before walking away.

Returning his attention to Dominic, Arturo frowned. "Ottavio seems to have issues with you these days," he said coolly. "He thinks you're not doing your job. Specifically, there seems to be more trouble in the territories I've assigned to you."

Dominic swallowed a surge of anger. Ottavio loved to make other high-ranking wolves look bad because he thought it made him look good, and he lived and died for Arturo's favor. "I don't care about Ottavio's opinions. I care about yours. Do *you* think I'm not doing my job?"

"If I thought that, there would be so many pieces of you, nobody could stitch them back together. But I have concerns. Many businesses have folded up shop. And there was the issue with the garbage collection. What have you found out so far?"

Dominic grimaced. Arturo wasn't going to like his answer. "The owner of the waste disposal company abandoned his business and left the city, just like the other business owners. I haven't been able to get any of them to speak to me yet. If we weren't facing this challenge from the Bianchi Pack, I'd suggest I get a special travel permit from the Mage's Council so I could go question them face to face and assure them no harm would come to them if they explained themselves. I was going to give you my report this morning, but then the call about the ghouls came in."

Arturo stared at Dominic, his gaze hard and searching. Finally, he gave a short, sharp nod. "Continue investigating. If you can't find answers soon …" he let his voice trail off without elaborating.

He headed over to his car and slid in the back. Ottavio and Carlo piled in the front, and they pulled away.

Dominic went to his car, where Romano was sitting behind the wheel. As they drove off, he felt a stirring of uneasiness. He didn't give a rat's ass what Ottavio thought, but Arturo was right; something was rotten in the city of Encantado, and that really said something.

CHAPTER TWELVE

Zoey glided to a stop in front of the warehouse on Lombard where Cin and her friends were staying now. She had a big box of pastries and a mission. Lorenzo was traveling to the Bianchi Pack's territory to hang out with Cin, and Zoey had to report back to Andrea that Lorenzo was all right.

Dominic had done yet another disappearing act, which made her nervous. She was constantly checking over her shoulder as she worked. She'd been in touch with Cin the whole time, and he hadn't seemed to be trying to track her down.

Cin, Lorenzo, and Heath were sitting on empty packing crates in front of the warehouse, waiting for her. A half-dozen kids gathered around a makeshift burn barrel stove, roasting squirrels on sticks. She didn't know their names, and sadly, the way new kids came and went all the time, half of them would probably be gone by next week. Cin and Heath had stuck around much longer than most.

She handed them the box of pastries, and they tore into them enthusiastically.

Cin, as usual, wore gorgeous new jewelry that looked out of place with her ragamuffin clothes. She couldn't possibly have afforded it on her own. Her necklace and earrings were dragons sculpted from silver wire. Little red flames accented the pieces.

"You have excellent taste in shoplifting," Zoey said to Cin.

"Mmmf fd bff cmfl," Cin replied around a mouthful of donut.

"Say what, girl who was raised in a barn?"

Cin swallowed and wiped her mouth with the back of her hand. "I said, you should be careful. Have you heard about the ghouls? Word on the street is that they ate some guy."

Zoey frowned. The street kids sometimes heard things before anybody else did. On the other hand, they loved gossip as much as any teenager, and it wasn't always accurate.

For instance, there were no killer mermaids eating people who boated on the pond at Greenwald Park.

"Wouldn't that be on the news?" Zoey quirked a brow.

"Not always. Sometimes the police hide it because they want to make sure poor people get eaten," Lorenzo said loftily.

"Says who?"

"Says Cin."

Cin nodded vigorously. She was already on her second donut. "My fremfs up norf tole me," she mumbled, crumbs falling out of her mouth.

"If ghouls are coming through the portal, maybe you guys should move farther south," Zoey said uneasily. It was possible the news had been suppressed so tourists wouldn't be scared off. It would be impossible to keep a full-blown ghoul attack under wraps, but an occasional ghoul slipping through the portal? They might be able to keep that quiet.

"Into the fancy areas? No way," Cin shook her head. "Too many cops."

"We'll be fine," Lorenzo said confidently. "If any ghouls come near us, I'll kick their skinny behinds." He reached into the pocket of his denim jacket and pulled out a pair of nunchucks.

"Do I want to know where you stole those from?" Zoey asked.

Lorenzo smirked. "I don't know, do you?"

Zoey tried to grab his donut from him, but he dodged her easily.

She made a clucking sound of disapproval. "Prison's not going to be as much fun as you think it is."

He smirked at her with all the confidence of a teenager who knows everything. "I run fast."

There was no point arguing with an infatuated kid who was trying to show off for his larcenous crush.

"Be careful. Lorenzo, you need to go home after this. Andrea is going to worry if you don't. I've got to go," Zoey said. "I've got a final job this evening. Peace out, juvenile delinquents from hell." Zoey climbed onto her bicycle.

"Later days, naggy old woman." Cin gave her a sarcastic mock salute.

Zoey clapped one hand to her chest in an exaggerated show of hurt. "Naggy, I will accept with pride. But *old woman?* How dare you. Just for that, stale donuts for a week. Not even kidding."

"Wait, you *are* kidding, right?" Heath called out after her. "Hey, I'm not the one who called you old! It was Cin! Cin gets the stale donuts, I get the good ones! Right?"

"Did you just throw me under the bus?" Cin elbowed Heath in the ribs.

He sidled away from her. "For fresh donuts? I'd throw you under a troll."

Zoey waved goodbye as she peddled away.

As she wove through traffic, she tried not to think about ghouls, which was about as effective as trying not to picture a pink elephant in a tutu. Would Cin and her friends be safe? What could she do to make them safer? Nothing, really. They were like semi-feral cats. She couldn't make them go stay in a foster home, where they chafed at having curfews and being treated like the kids they were. The local authorities had enough on their plate dealing with semi-regular magic attacks. They wouldn't be bothered trying to corral a group of throwaway kids.

There was a package already waiting for her at the dispatch center. She had no idea what was inside, and she didn't ask. Stuffing it in her bag, she zipped across town to the restaurant. Well, she was reasonably zippy. There were more obstacles than usual in her path—there had been ever since that whole weird wolf thing with Dominic. Was that just a coincidence? She was getting so used to it now, she barely even noticed and went whichever way the little GPS in her head told her. The obstacles often moved with her, trying to cut her off, which almost certainly meant they were related to Dominic.

Even with the detours, Zoey made it to the restaurant fifteen minutes early. It was a little hole in the wall Italian joint, her favorite kind, and as she walked in, the smells made her stomach growl.

The restaurant was packed, but she had been directed to go to a small room in the back. She pushed open a creaky wooden door and stepped into what seemed to be an empty room. A half-dozen tables with red and white checked plastic table clothes and flickering votive candles took up the space. As she stepped into the room, someone shut the door, and when she spun around to see who it was, she bumped right into Dominic. Wearing a pinstriped suit and a pale-blue silk shirt that made his eyes look even more beautiful, he stood between her and the door.

"You," she said, clutching the package to her chest and taking a quick two steps back. "What a surprise."

He feigned a hurt expression. "Is that any way to greet your mate after a hard day's work?"

"No," she said, eyes sparking with annoyance. "That is definitely not how I'd greet my mate. Or husband, as we human-types say."

Amusement lit his eyes. "Sassy. Don't you want to know what's in the package? It's for you."

"For me?" she said, startled.

"Open it!"

Zoey was tempted to say something snarky, but the look on Dominic's face was so expectant and hopeful, she just couldn't.

"Thank you," she said grudgingly, tearing at the wrapping. Then she hesitated. "Is this something kinky or weird? It's not handcuffs, is it?"

"No, I keep those in my bedroom." He winked. "Along with some other toys."

Dammit. Why did he have to go and say that? Her heartbeat sped up and she felt damp in her girly parts.

He sniffed the air appreciatively. "You like handcuffs." He nodded approvingly. "Good to know."

"Stop … stop doing that!" she sputtered, blushing so hard her face hurt. But she also really loved getting presents, and she hardly ever got them these days, so she ripped open the package and something spilled out in a river of glorious green silk. Her favorite color. She held up the stunning evening gown.

"For you," he said. "You can change in the restroom. Or right here. Preferably right here. You're having dinner with me."

Zoey was about to lie and say she wasn't hungry, but her traitorous stomach growled. She clapped her hand over it, as if that would help. "What about my bike?"

"I'll have it brought inside and Sergio will keep it in the back for you."

Was this when he'd claim her and take her back to the pack compound? Damn her overactive libido. She had the chance to ask him as many questions as she'd wanted, and she'd blown it. She'd been dying to ask him exactly when this claiming would happen.

So she could hide.

"Promise you'll let me go afterward?"

"If you want to go, you can go."

Zoey snorted. "I'm holding you to that." Right. She could talk tough, but if Dominic wanted to drag her back to his lair, it wasn't as if she could actually do anything about it.

She went into the bathroom and pulled out her phone and used the app that notified her boss she'd delivered her package and was off for the night.

Stripping off her sweaty jeans and t-shirt, she slid the dress on. With a grimace of dismay, she remembered she didn't have shoes to go with the dress, so she was wearing big clunky sneakers.

She was so hungry she could eat a hippo, so she threw back her shoulders and strode out of the bathroom, trying to fake a confidence she didn't feel at all.

"Are you sure I look ... okay?" She gestured at the dress awkwardly.

He looked her up and down. "Okay? No. Not at all." He shook his head. "Not okay."

Zoey felt as if she'd been punched in the stomach. She hadn't realized how much she cared about Dominic's opinion until he said those cruel words. And she realized she'd foolishly started to trust him in a way—she thought he'd never hurt her feelings.

The next thing she knew, her back was up against the wall, and Dominic was pressed up against her. The thick length of his erection pressed into her stomach, and he was breathing hard.

"Okay?" he repeated. "You never look just *okay*. You look good enough to fucking eat. And believe me, that's going to happen in a very short time. Dinner, dessert, you. Possibly in that order."

"Me?" she squeaked. "But I ... my hair's a mess, my face is sunburned ..."

He tangled his fingers in her shiny brown hair. "I know," he said approvingly. "You look like you just rolled out of my bed. Bedhead hair, your face kissed by the sun ..."

"Wow," she murmured. "You are very good at putting a positive spin on things."

"I only speak the truth."

He was bending down to kiss her when the door banged open, and the delicious smell of garlic wafted in. A roly-poly man in a chef's apron and chef's white cap bustled through the door carrying a tray of pasta dishes. He had a droopy dark mustache and looked as if he should be the advertisement for a line of spaghetti sauce.

"Oh, I interrupt!" he said in a heavy Italian accent, his eyes going wide.

"Yes, you do, Sergio," Dominic grumbled.

Zoey squirmed in his arms, embarrassed, and tried to push him away, but it was like pushing a building.

"You want dinner, or you no want dinner?" Sergio looked comically offended. "I spend hours in the kitchen, over a hot stove, for you! You come to my house, you eat! *Mangia, mangia!*" He set the dishes on a table, next to a bowl of bread and a bottle of wine.

Dominic reluctantly released Zoey, and the two of them walked over to the table. Dominic pulled out the chair for her to sit down, and she tried to remember if any man had ever done that before.

"Enjoy!" Sergio said. "And Dominic? You treat this gorgeous girl right or I steal her!"

Dominic growled. Sergio backed up, eyes widening. "I kid, I kid!"

"Settle down," Zoey said to Dominic, although she was secretly the teeniest bit flattered. Nobody had ever been jealous of her before.

Dominic poured her a glass of excellent red wine. They dove into the food, and her linguine with shrimp and lemon butter was what she would have requested for a last meal. It was heaven on a plate. The garlic butter was soft and fluffy and tangy. For once, she didn't feel self-conscious eating in front of a man. He'd told her he loved her body just the way it was, and she believed him.

They ate in companionable silence, taking their time, enjoying the food. She didn't feel pressured to make idle chit chat; she just savored every bite.

Zoey smiled as she set down her fork to take another sip of

wine, and Dominic nodded. "Smiling is good. Better than running from me. Tell me what you're thinking."

"It's nice to be able to relax and forget life's stresses sometimes."

"I can make all of your stresses disappear." She arched an eyebrow, and he grinned fiercely. "You're about to say, 'So you'll disappear, Dominic?'"

"Damn, am I already becoming predictable?" She shook her head ruefully and finished her glass of wine.

Dominic poured her another, and then reached out and took her hand. "I'd rather say reliable. Look at us, sparring like an old married couple already." His hand was so big it engulfed hers, warm and comfortable like a blanket. He grinned, flashing big white teeth.

She let him hold her hand for a minute. It felt so good to sit there with a handsome man who looked at her with lust in his eyes even after she'd just carbo-loaded enough pasta to feed a medium-sized orc.

"Damn, Sergio really is an amazing cook. He's single, you say?"

Dominic narrowed his eyes at her, and his growl rumbled in his broad chest.

"Seriously." She shook her head in wonder. "Are you actually jealous?"

"Well, the man does know his way around a plate of pasta. Some women like that in a mate," he huffed.

"Yes. That is pretty hot," she agreed just to torture him. Then, because the growl was getting louder and she didn't want him to kill a man who made the best Italian food she'd ever tasted, she quickly said, "Tell me more about this moon-bite thing you keep hallucinating about."

"Come back to my house with me and we'll discuss it." He gave her hand a gentle squeeze.

"You keep saying that like I have a choice." She narrowed her eyes at him. "Do I have a choice?"

Dominic avoided her gaze, released her hand, and stabbed into his plate of pasta.

"Ah, a loophole. Does this have something to do with that twenty-eight days thing you talked about?" she mused. "Do I have a choice until the next full moon?"

His handsome brows drew together in a scowl. "Maybe."

"Can I say no to the whole thing at any time?"

"Can you reject my wolf's claim? Nope." He pinned her with a fierce glower. "Do you want to?"

She flushed. "That's a complicated question. I barely know you, and … as we discussed, you and I have very different viewpoints on things."

"You were upset with us because you thought we were taking your neighborhood's money and not giving you what you'd paid for. Understandable. But now you know differently."

"Yes, and I'm really relieved to know that, but that's not the only thing. There's also your … methods of enforcement."

"We defend ourselves when attacked?" he said mildly.

"By killing people. And you extort money from businesses!"

"We give them protection the police can't. If we didn't protect them, they'd be targets of curses from competitors, ghouls, or ogres. We are willing to die to protect any business that pays us our fee."

She was running out of arguments. "You encourage gambling," she mumbled.

"Ahh. Like in Las Vegas?"

Zoey hated how he was batting away every argument and making it seem as if they were an organization of benevolent businessmen. They weren't! But … were they really that bad? Especially compared to everyone else who ran this lousy corrupt city? Dammit. How was he getting inside her head like this?

She sighed and reluctantly set her fork on her plate. The buttery taste of pasta lingered on her taste buds, and she ran her tongue along her lips. The air suddenly felt warm, and she realized Dominic was watching her with a fierce hunger that burned away all of her defenses and nearly set her panties on fire.

I need to nip this in the bud.

She cleared her throat and squirmed in her seat. "All right, let's discuss this logically. It makes no sense that you would want to hitch yourself to me forever. I mean, wolves mate for life. You don't know me at all."

His eyes gleamed with amusement. The more she resisted, the more it seemed to arouse him. "We have all the time in the world to get to know each other."

"And before your wolf bit me on the ass, you never even

noticed me." Her voice was higher than she'd meant it to be, and she realized there was a shrill undercurrent of hurt to it. She winced in embarrassment, but Dominic didn't seem to notice.

"The first time you catered one of our events, you wore your hair piled up in a messy bun." Dominic's voice was grave, and for once, that fierce gleam of humor faded and he was dead serious. "The sun lit up your hair and made it look like rich caramel. You wore little wire earrings with red stone hearts."

He'd noticed all that?

Zoey thought her heart would stop. His gaze met hers, seizing it and holding it captive.

"I don't have them anymore. My friend Cin gave me those. She stole them from somewhere, and when I figured that out, I made her take them back."

"No, she made them. She makes jewelry."

"She does? How do you know that?" And why did *she* not know that? When she'd asked Cin if she'd stolen the earrings, Cin had just shrugged and said, "I couldn't exactly afford to buy them, could I?"

She felt a pang of embarrassment. Her plate was always too full, working two jobs, volunteering, and trying to keep their neighborhood from falling apart. She'd let herself get distracted and now she was making snap judgments, which was kind of a way of putting up a wall between her and Cin.

Cin was hard and prickly and also frighteningly reckless.

If Zoey didn't get close to Cin, she wouldn't have to worry about her as much, right? But that wasn't fair. Cin needed someone to worry about her. No matter how busy Zoey was, she should have found a way to spend more time with the street kids and get to know them. Maybe then she wouldn't have been so judgy.

Dominic reached out across the table and took her hand in his, his lips curling in a cruel smile. "Knowing things is my business." His voice carried a dark, sensual undercurrent, a veiled threat and promise that mingled together and snatched her breath away.

She looked at him skeptically. "Are you saying you were interested in me from the first minute you saw me?"

"Entranced is how I'd describe it. I saw how you carried yourself with confidence and faced down mafia bosses even though you were quaking inside. I saw how kind you were to Carlo when he couldn't figure out how to tie his own shoelace. You just knelt down and laced it up for him and talked about the weather like it was no big deal. And then you showed him how to do it himself without making him feel foolish. Ever since then, he's remembered. When you were in the back with the other girls taking a break, you grew flowers and stuck them in a glass of water and made that dingy little break room feel like a party. And you made sure everyone had something to eat before you started."

He took a bite of pasta, casually chewing as if he hadn't just tossed a bomb at her that blew up her entire world. This was even more life-altering than hearing his wolf had claimed her as a mate. Now he was saying he had actually wanted her all along.

"So why did you never make a move on me?" Zoey's heart thudded in her chest. She wanted to believe. More than anything. Not because she could ever let herself have a man like Dominic—a hardened criminal with walls around him she'd never breach—but just because it was the most marvelous, magical thing a man had ever said to her.

"Because, as one of the highest-ranking men serving under Arturo Moretti, I am expected to mate for the good of the pack and make a political alliance, not for love or desire. Unless my wolf chooses otherwise." He took a sip of wine. "Your turn. What did you notice about me when you first saw me?"

Zoey tilted her head to the side. "You were very handsome, and very self-confident, but not in a flashy way. A lot of the made wolves carry themselves like they have something to prove. You didn't. You were also very alone. You stood back and watched everybody but didn't let anyone get close to you."

"Romano's usually right by my side."

"Physically. Mentally and emotionally, you're a million miles away from him. And everyone else."

He poked at the remains of the pasta on his plate but didn't reply. The lights in the restaurant flickered.

"Restaurant's getting ready to close."

"Kind of early, isn't it?" she said, puzzled. It was just starting to get dark.

"We're near a vamp area."

"Ahh. That's right, I forgot."

Lone humans and low-level magic-bloods tended to disappear from vamp areas at night. Rent near vamp areas was super cheap, although the price of garlic was through the roof. It also explained why an Italian restaurant would have set up shop in this neighborhood; a meal here would guarantee a person a safe walk home.

He put down his spoon. "You haven't had dessert. I own this building, and I have an apartment upstairs where I crash sometimes. Come upstairs, and if you want to leave afterwards, I will escort you home myself."

"That's a terrible idea," she grumbled, and she kept repeating that to herself as she let him lead her by the hand from the restaurant and up a flight of stairs by the side of the building.

Georgette St Clair

CHAPTER THIRTEEN

Dominic's apartment took up the entire floor above the restaurant. The furniture was black leather and rich cherrywood. There were framed watercolors of Nevada landscapes on the walls. Zoey recognized some of them by a well-known local artist. The bookshelf against the wall was beautifully arranged, with hardcover art, photography books, and bronze sculptures of wolves.

She never would have guessed his apartment would look so warm and homey. She'd pictured something sterile and straight out of a catalog. What else didn't she know about him?

"You support the arts," she murmured, pausing to look at a watercolor and admiring the luscious jewel tones of a desert sunset.

As he shed his suit jacket, he gave her a wry smile with an oddly wistful undertone. "Does that get me points?"

"It doesn't detract any," she said grudgingly.

"Wow. Tough crowd." He took off his tie and unbuttoned the top few buttons of his shirt, but he didn't move closer to her—yet.

"More wine?" Dominic headed to the kitchen, and she followed.

The kitchen was decorated in a modern art deco style with bright reds, yellows, and blues, and there were even more paintings on the walls in there. Absentmindedly, she stroked a drooping basil plant, letting her earth energy flow into it, and it sprang back to life.

"I'm fine, thanks. Oh, and thank you for an amazing dinner. I loved that restaurant," she said. "I'm curious though. Your pack owns a restaurant at the Arena. Why didn't you take me there?"

"I thought it was too loud and flashy. I didn't want to overwhelm you."

"That's surprisingly thoughtful."

"I'm full of surprises. Some of them are even good ones. Like the neighborhood garden center. And this tiramisu." He pulled open the refrigerator door.

Zoey was sure she was too full for dessert, but when he served her up a plate of the creamy confection, she suddenly found room.

He only had one rule: he had to feed it to her. She should have said no, but then she wouldn't get any tiramisu. And she really wanted the tiramisu.

He moved the kitchen chairs so he was sitting next to her and spoon fed her bite after bite of the meltingly sweet dessert until the bowl was empty.

"Seconds?" he offered.

"You know what I want more than dessert? Information about you. And don't try to distract me by asking for a kiss first. I'm wise to you and your addictive lips."

He set the fork on the plate and drew his brows together. "What kind of things do you want to know?"

"Why are you so reluctant to share anything about yourself with me?"

Dominic stood, grabbing her empty bowl, and carried it to the sink before he answered. "I'm a private kind of person."

"Why would you think I'd want to share my life with someone who won't share anything of himself with me? You know all about me, and I know nothing about you. It hardly seems fair."

His lip curled in that cruel smile of his. "I never fight fair."

Usually, Zoey found his smile terrifying and sexy in equal measure. Right now, she found it infuriating. She shoved back her chair and stood abruptly, her eyes flashing with anger.

"All right! I'm sorry," Dominic said, leaning against the sink. "I know, I can be kind of defensive. Ask me something. One question. I'll answer, whatever it is."

She sat back down. Only one question? There were so many

things she wanted to know about him. "Why did you decide to get bitten by a warrior-class wolf? What made it worth the risk?" she blurted out, then bit her lip. There were so many other things she could have asked.

His gaze took on a faraway look. "What risk? I didn't have anyone who'd miss me."

"I'm sorry," she said quietly. Perhaps she had asked the right question after all. That gave her surprising insight into his life but raised a million more questions.

"No reason to be." He grabbed a bottle from the wine rack on the kitchen counter. As he poured, the phone rang with her mother's ringtone. Zoey quickly silenced it.

He snapped to attention. "Who's that?"

"Nobody."

He set a glass of wine on the table. "Nobody, like some guy who wants to take you out on a date?" His voice had become dark and dangerous.

"It's my mom, okay?" she said, exasperated. "Nobody wants to take me out on a date. Except some crazy wolf who won't take no for an answer and expects me to marry him without knowing a damned thing about him!"

"Why don't you answer her?" He arched an eyebrow. "Unless it's actually not your mom?"

The phone started ringing again, and he lunged for it. She shoved it down the front of her dress. He threw back his head and roared with laughter.

"Oh, Zoey, of all the places for you to hide it … thank you for that."

She stood and leapt back, but Dominic was on her in a flash, pinning her up against the wall. When the phone rang again, he grabbed the front of her dress and ripped it open as if it were wet tissue paper.

A split second later, he had grabbed the phone. Nimbly dodging her, he answered it.

"Hello, Zoey's mother. Lucinda, is that right?"

Zoey didn't have more than a micro-second to freak out about the fact he knew her mother's name.

"Who is this?" she heard her mother's voice.

She lunged for the phone, but he danced back, holding it tauntingly over his head. Then he whirled around, his back to her.

"Oh, Zoey didn't tell you about me? My name is Dominic Lombardi."

"I need to talk to Zoey, please. I've been trying to reach her and she hasn't answered." Her mother sounded irritated and worried. Dammit. That was last thing Zoey needed.

"Of course, ma'am, just one minute and I'll get her." Oh, it was ma'am now? Suddenly, he was mister polite, respectful choirboy.

He covered the phone with his hand. "What will you give me not to tell her I mate-bit your ass?" he whispered.

"I won't kill you!" she hissed furiously.

A chortle rumbled up from deep inside him. "Yeah, that's kind of a given. So? What do I get?"

"You bastard!" Zoey grabbed at the phone, and he danced back out of her reach again.

"Zoey?" her mother called out.

"One more kiss!" she whispered desperately.

Dominic smiled in triumph and handed her the phone. She was so going to murder him. He was going to be very, very dead.

"Mother!" she said brightly. "I'm fine!"

"Why weren't you answering the phone? I was worried!"

"I was in the restroom."

"Are you on a date? Who is that man?"

She winced. Such a loaded question. "He's a businessman." Not a total lie. "He works in security. We've, ah, been out a few times."

"You're not at his house, are you?" Great, the mom morality police was on patrol.

Dominic was listening to every word with his hand pressed over his mouth, his shoulders shaking from quiet laughter. Zoey's face flushed red and she glared bloody murder at him.

"Mother! Of course not. I'm at a restaurant."

"What kind of restaurant? It's very quiet," her mother replied suspiciously.

"They're about to close," Zoey said desperately. "He's going to give me a ride home. You don't have to worry. He always walks me to the door and makes sure I make it inside safely."

"Well, he does sound like a gentleman. And the fact you told him my name must mean this is something serious." Her mother's tone of voice suddenly was warm with approval. What had just happened?

Dominic smirked, and Zoey gave him the finger.

"Well, it's early days," she said brightly while waving her hand with the middle finger still extended.

"My intentions for your daughter are entirely honorable!" Dominic blurted out. "I look forward to meeting your family next time you visit. She's told me so much about you. Congratulations on that tournament, by the way. Go Tigers!" The Tigers were the mascot for her youngest brother's middle school. How the hell did he know about that?

"Mother, we do need to go now. I'll call you tomorrow, okay?"

"Do call me," her mother said severely.

"Mrs. Monroe, I will make sure of it!" Dominic called out just before Zoey hung up.

"You!" she yelled at him. She dropped her phone into her purse on the kitchen table and pummeled his chest with her fists. It hurt her hands, so she stopped. He was laughing so hard, he had to wipe tears from his cheeks.

"Oh my God. Wow. That was the best-timed phone call ever."

She put her hands on her hips. "Just go ahead and kiss me so I can go home already."

"I get to pick where I kiss you."

"For heaven's sake!"

He must mean the bedroom.

She stalked into the bedroom, the front of her dress hanging open where he'd ripped it.

The bed had a chrome steel framework and silky black and silver pillows piled on a silvery comforter. Moody black-and-white photographs of modern architecture adorned the walls.

He walked in behind her, still smirking.

"What's so funny?" she demanded.

"I didn't mean what *room*. I meant I get to pick where on *your body* I kiss you. And for how long."

"What?" she took a step backward. "That's not fair!"

"I believe we've established I never fight fair. Are you going to keep your word?"

No. "Yes," she breathed.

He knelt on the ground and lifted her gown, revealing her pale-pink cotton underwear. He pressed his lips against them with reverence and breathed in as if she smelled like a field of roses.

To her shock, he stood and looped his arms around her waist.

"How are you doing, Zoey Monroe?"

"I … I'm all right."

"You miss your parents, don't you? You should let them come visit you more often."

A sudden flood of emotion washed over her. "It can be dangerous here. I'd rather they stay where it's safe."

"Always taking care of other people's needs, aren't you?" His voice had become quiet and serious.

"I …" Her face flushed. Just when she'd managed to convince herself he was an insensitive jerk, he had to go and say something like that. Like he really cared about her on a very deep level.

She cleared her throat. "I mean … it makes me happy to help other people. I want to see the people I care about do well."

"Nothing wrong with that. But if they have needs, can't you have them too? Who takes care of your needs, Zoey?"

The words dried up in her throat.

"What do you need right now?"

"I don't know," she confessed. She could have said something snarky—like she needed to go home—but she couldn't bring herself to lash out at Dominic when he exposed his tender side.

She really didn't know what she needed. Once upon a time, she'd thought she needed to leave Encantado, but she had good friends there. They couldn't leave, so even if she could, she wouldn't leave them behind. It was scary. Navigating life in a portal city could be frustrating and challenging, but it was also magical and fascinating.

"I don't know anymore," she said again, a sudden weariness pressing down on her.

"You look tense. I think what you need is a backrub."

His hands on her body, rubbing all the stress out? She shivered and hugged herself, and it took all of her strength to keep from squealing in excitement. "Well, I wouldn't absolutely hate it."

Dominic pretended to look hurt. "Wow. Don't get overexcited about it."

Zoey struggled for a snappy comeback, but the words died in her throat.

She let him strip off her clothing, and then he led her over to the bed where she laid face down.

He straddled her and rustled around in the nightstand. A minute later, she felt oil dripping onto her back. Dominic began kneading her back with his strong hands, and she moaned in pleasure. It went on and on as he squeezed and rubbed the tension from her muscles. She could feel her body melting into the mattress. She couldn't have moved if all the ghouls in Encantado were swarming into her room.

Finally, he slid off the bed, taking off his clothes and folding them neatly and setting them on top of his dresser as she watched. And what a view. Broad chest, a six-pack that looked as if it had been carved in marble, a dark thatch of pubic hair, and a thick erect cock that rested against his stomach as it pointed straight up at the ceiling.

Dominic walked over to the bed … closer, closer … her breath caught in her throat.

He laid next to her and … took her in his arms.

"Goodnight, Zoey," he said, kissing her lips very lightly.

His erection pressed into her thigh, but he didn't make a move. She lay there, lightheaded with desire, feeling his chest rise and fall.

Finally, she cleared her throat. "That's it?" she said. "You could … I mean …" Dammit, was he going to make her beg?

"Nope," he said stubbornly. "I am going to show you I want you for much more than your gorgeous body. I wanted to spend time with you tonight just to be with you. And that's what we're going to do, no matter how much pain I'm in from restraining myself."

"And how much pain is that exactly?" Zoey hoped it was a lot because she ached so hard for him, she wanted to grab an ice pack and shove it between her legs.

"On a scale of one to infinity? Infinity squared." Then he grumbled. "You don't have to smile quite so loudly."

"You cannot hear me smile!" she protested.

"I have mad skills, sweetheart. Over time, you will learn about all of them."

They laid like that for hours. He was too stubborn to make the first move, and she was too proud to beg.

Finally, Zoey gave in. "Dammit, you stubborn ass. If you don't have sex with me right now, I am going to make you regret it."

"I thought you'd never ask."

"You thought I'd never– You son of a bitch!" she shrieked and punched him on the arm. She'd forgotten how solid he was. "Ouch, damn you!"

In one swift move, Dominic slid on top of her, his heavy weight pinning her to the mattress. "True, but I'm the bastard who's going to be your mate."

He began feathering her with soft kisses, his lips brushing ever so lightly over her skin.

"I love your freckles," he murmured, pressing his mouth against the dots. She shivered in pleasure.

He kissed her neck, working his way down to her breasts. Cupping her breast in his hand, he suckled the ruby tips, nipping at them gently.

"Oh," she gasped. "That feels … oh."

"Yes, it does, doesn't it?" He trailed kisses down her soft stomach, and for the first time in her life, she had no temptation whatsoever to suck it in.

He slid down so his face was between her thighs and spread her legs roughly.

"Mine," he growled into her pussy and claimed it with a long, slow stroke of his tongue. Zoey sucked in a gasp of pleasure as he lapped at her, her thighs quivering under the strong grip of his hands.

Hot pleasure swirled through her body, and she felt light as air. Was that her voice urging him on shamelessly? It must have been. Dominic responded by thrusting his tongue inside her and fucking her with it as he stroked her stiff, aching clit with one hand.

Zoey tangled her fingers in his silky hair as he pleasured her, and sensation built inside her until she was ready to peak. Dominic slid away, the heat and sweetness of the moment vanishing.

"Dominic!" she cried out.

"Are you my mate?"

"You bastard!"

"Are you?" He moved up, straddling her and trapping her between his thighs.

"Yes!" she choked out.

Dominic grinned in triumph and adjusted his hips, placing the head of his cock against her entrance. Zoey cried out as he thrusted into her. He was too big, stretching her, and she loved it.

He pumped into her hard and fast, his breath harsh and guttural in her ear. Several times he paused, and she grabbed his ass and urged him on. He chuckled quietly.

"Just need … oh God … to be sure you want it as much as me … oh, you're so fucking tight and wet for me … oh my God …"

The dam broke, and the waves of pleasure washed over her in a tsunami of sensation. Zoey came hard, her muscles spasming and gripping his cock. Dominic's answering cry of pleasure sent a jolt of triumph through her. They were so tightly wrapped up in each other as they found their release, it was impossible to tell where one ended and the other began.

CHAPTER FOURTEEN

Zoey woke up to the smell of coffee and pancakes.
Not the worst way to be greeted by a new day.

She padded into the kitchen dressed in the extra set of clothes she carried in her messenger bag—jeans and a t-shirt, her usual work uniform. Dominic was ridiculously sexy in plaid boxer shorts as he flipped pancakes onto a plate. He turned and smiled at her when she walked in.

She grabbed a mug and poured a cup of coffee, added some cream from the pitcher, and took a sip.

"You do make a mean cup of coffee, Dominic. My friend Danielle would like you."

"Danielle's a woman, right?" His jealous tone was back.

"Is that a serious question?" She laughed.

"I don't know. It could be French. Like, the French pronunciation of Daniel." He set a stack fluffy pancakes in front of her.

"Do hear yourself?" She sipped deeply from her mug. "You've apparently dug into my background and my entire life. You should know by now, I'm a one-man-at-a-time kind of girl." Zoey grabbed the jug of maple syrup and poured it on her pancakes.

"And I'm that one man," Dominic said firmly.

She winked at him. "For the time being." She enjoyed his groan of frustration. He was really fun to torture.

"By the way, love the tattoo," he said. "Right next to my mate-bite scar. 'Love bites'? It's like it was meant to be."

"Huh," she said. "Never thought of it that way." He looked so pleased with himself, she had to laugh.

After the best breakfast she'd had in ages, Zoey got her spell phone from her messenger bag and called the dispatch center to let them know she was available.

Dominic frowned. Pushing back his chair, he strolled over to her and gathered her into his arms. She leaned into him, loving the feeling of his broad, muscular chest.

"You could stay a little longer," he murmured, stroking a lock of hair from her face.

It sounded so tempting, which was why she had to leave. She'd never meant to spend the night, wonderful as it had been. Yes, he was great at sex, made her feel really good about herself, and he was a gentleman in all things. He held doors open for her, he made sure she came first, and often, he brought her snacks in bed. He was all about her pleasure and comfort.

She still felt as if he were a mystery wrapped in an enigma, as if everything she knew about him was on the surface. She didn't know what made Dominic Lombardi tick.

He didn't seem to know how to take things slowly. He'd barreled into her life and demanded … everything. Maybe that's how it worked with wolves, but she was human and didn't believe in love at first bite.

Zoey still needed time to think and make sense of all this, so she needed to get out of here while she still had the willpower to do so.

"I can't stay any longer, thanks," she said. "Breakfast was amazing. You were amazing. Unfortunately, I need to give myself some extra time to get to work. I'm sensing obstacles."

"Sensing … what? I thought you were a garden witch." He looked puzzled.

Oh crud. Apparently, he didn't know *everything* about her, and she'd like to keep it that way. If he didn't know about her map skills, that made it easier to hide from him.

"Yep. Sure am. You are not wrong." She tried to wriggle out of his arms.

He tightened his grip around her waist. "Tell me more."

She tried to duck, but now he had her caged too tightly. Her struggles were having an effect on him; she could feel that effect—long and thick and hard—pressing into her stomach. If this went on much longer, she'd lose all motivation to leave.

"I can wait all day," he murmured into her hair.

She tipped up her head and glared. "You are an absolute jerkoff!"

He smiled down at her. "I'm having fun. How about you?"

She scowled. "I'm going to be late."

"What a shame."

Zoey let out a hiss of frustration. She'd already lost the job working for Kalinda; she couldn't afford to lose the bike messenger job too.

"Fine! I'm also a map witch. Let go of me."

He released her. "What is that?"

"I have a connection to the earth, and because of it, I can find my way around pretty well." He arched an eyebrow. "Okay, I can find my way just about anywhere. I can also sense obstacles. And the problem is, I'm sensing a lot more obstacles these days, all over town."

Dominic's brow wrinkled. "What kind of obstacles are you running into?"

She shrugged. "I don't know. My magic doesn't tell me that. It could be a traffic jam, a rampaging troll, road construction … my magic just lets me know where things will either slow me down or stop me completely."

Dominic's muscles bunched with tension. "That can't be a coincidence. We have enemies. We're in a feud with the Bianchi Pack. They are strictly forbidden from interfering with females, but … I don't trust them. Come stay with us. I can keep you safe."

"Do I still have a choice?"

Dominic hesitated before saying "yes" with great reluctance.

"Then no," she sighed. "If I go with you, I'm afraid I'd never get to leave. And I still have a life, Dominic."

That earned her a scowl. "At the next full moon …"

Zoey met his gaze coolly. "You underestimate my abilities, Dominic."

His eyes filled with dark possessiveness. "And you overestimate my patience."

Before she could say anything else, there was a knock on the door. Dominic's expression went sour with annoyance.

"Dammit. Romano has the worst damn timing." He stalked off to answer the door just as her phone beeped with a text message from Danielle.

"R U boinking a Moretti Pack member???"

Zoey hurried into the bathroom so she could speak in privacy and called her friend. Danielle answered on the first thing.

"What the hell?" Danielle demanded.

"It's complicated! Dominic Lombardi's wolf bit me on a full moon. Apparently, that means he thinks I'm his mate."

"Then tell him you're not!" Danielle sounded appalled.

"Gee, why didn't I think of that?" Zoey said, annoyed. "He's Moretti Pack, Danielle, and he claimed me publicly."

"You mean, you're going with it?"

Was she? Zoey hesitated. "He's … not what I thought he was."

"Do you know why all the businesses have been closing up? I found out. Everyone's talking about it. It's the Moretti Pack. The pack deliberately raised their protection fees so high, they couldn't stay in business anymore, and lots of the business owners are just leaving the city so the Moretti Pack can't murder them. People are spending their life savings just to escape them. They're ruining the city, Zoey. Please tell me you're not okay with that."

Zoey felt an odd flare of protectiveness toward Dominic. Where had that come from?

"Come on, Danielle, those are just rumors. We all thought it was the Moretti Pack behind the garbage problem, and it turned out it was just a corrupt neighborhood liaison. The pack took care of it. Why would they force businesses to shut down? Then they couldn't collect money from them. That would hurt the pack, not help them."

"Spoken like someone who's got a rich new boyfriend and is forgetting who her real friends are. You never used to come up with excuses for them. If you'll excuse me, I'm going to go walk twenty blocks to the nearest coffee shop. You have fun playing mobster's mate." Danielle hung up on her.

Frustrated, Zoey stalked out of the bathroom. Dominic shot a sour look at Romano as he served himself pancakes. Romano waved cheerily at her.

"Romano, we've got to stop meeting like this," Zoey said.

"Yeah, yeah. And you guys didn't have sex." Romano gave her an exaggerated wink.

She brushed him off with a wave and turned her attention to Dominic.

"What do you know about all the businesses closing in our neighborhood? They're just disappearing. They pay protection money to the Moretti Pack, right? You must be keeping track of them."

The warmth in his eyes vanished. It was as if a door had slammed shut in her face. "We don't speak of pack business to non-pack members."

She felt as if someone had dumped a bucket of ice water on her head. Who was this man? One minute he was inviting her in, letting her see little pieces of himself, and making her feel as if she were special and magical. The next minute, he was everything she'd hated and feared from the minute she'd arrived in Encantado.

The other Dominic made her melt like butter on a hot sunny day. But this cold, hard stranger standing in front of her? She would not be the mate, or wife, of this man.

"I see," she said tightly. "I see a lot. Things I really don't want to see. Thanks for last night. It was … interesting." She flung the verbal shrapnel right in his face, and he flinched. Good. She'd meant it to hurt because she felt like he'd just punched her in the stomach.

Holding her messenger bag, she turned around and walked into the bedroom before shutting and locking the door behind her.

"Zoey!" Dominic bellowed, his voice so loud the door shook.

She shot out the window and onto the fire escape just as he kicked in the bedroom door with a sound like a bomb going off.

Scrambling down the ladder, she dropped to the ground with a painful thud and disappeared around the corner. She'd leave her bike at Sergio's for now; she had another bike stashed in an empty warehouse in the warehouse district. Dominic was about to learn how hard it was to track down a map witch who didn't want to be found.

CHAPTER FIFTEEN

Zoey muttered curses under her breath as she glided to a stop in front of her building. It had taken twice as long to get here because obstacles had popped up in front of her everywhere she went.

She'd been hiding from Dominic for a week and had only come back because she needed to pick up some clothes. Ever since she'd stormed out of Dominic's apartment, she hadn't gone to work and had drained most of her funds. Luckily, she'd been able to crash in an abandoned building on the east side and found food using her dumpster-diving skills.

She also intended to make Danielle talk to her, whether Danielle wanted to or not, which was why she'd brought coffee with her. She wasn't above bribery.

She stepped off her bicycle, trying to determine what was different about her neighborhood. Then it hit her: it didn't reek of garbage.

The air was sweet and fresh; it smelled like a walk through a flower garden.

At least Dominic had kept his word.

Still feeling gloomy, she went to Danielle's apartment and rapped on the door until Danielle answered. It was only noon, way before Danielle liked to wake up.

When Danielle opened the door, Zoey shoved the cup of coffee at her. Danielle grabbed the cup and took a swig, letting out a sigh of appreciation.

"You look awful." Danielle looked Zoey up and down. "I thought your new gangster boyfriend would pay for you to go to a salon and dress you in designer clothes. So he's not just a criminal, he's a cheapskate?"

"Gee, I missed this." Zoey elbowed past her into the living room and flopped onto the couch. "I asked Dominic about what's happening with the local businesses. He wouldn't answer me, so I left and haven't spoken to him since. I haven't been able to go to work or stay in my apartment because he'd be able to find me. And it's not my fault his wolf bit me on a full moon and now he thinks he's stuck with me."

Danielle took another sip of coffee. "Well, you did bring me caffeine," she said grudgingly. "I'm sorry he makes you feel like he's stuck with you. Sounds like a douche."

Zoey sighed. "Okay, in fairness, he doesn't really make me feel like he's stuck with me. According to him, it's more like some kind of weird fate thing. He's very flattering, and he's the only guy I've ever met who's ever made me feel like an actual fairy princess. He's kind of a moody dick … and very stalkery."

Danielle tilted her head to the side. "Like, sexy rom-com stalkery, or restraining order stalkery?"

"Umm, well, I—"

"The first one," Danielle interrupted drily. "He isn't terrible to look at, I guess … for a criminal. What are you going to do?"

"He's got this idea he can claim me on the next full moon. I was thinking, maybe if that date comes and goes, he's not allowed to claim me after all?"

Danielle just gave her a skeptical look and finished her coffee. "And when that inevitably fails?"

"Wow, such crushing pessimism! I've *really* missed this!" At Danielle's sour side-eye, Zoey laughed. "No, I really have, and I haven't thought that far ahead yet. I've just decided to believe it'll work. Now, do you know if there are any pack members upstairs in my apartment?"

"Nah, but they've been watching the building from the

apartment across the street. You're in the clear today though. They left about an hour ago because there was a report of ghouls in the northwest. They made it into a subdivision and ate a mailman."

"Yikes. Poor guy. I'd better hurry and get my stuff."

Zoey raced upstairs and packed some clean clothing. When she came back down, she knocked on Danielle's door again so she could say goodbye.

"So you're just going to go back to sleeping in a squat for the next two weeks?" Danielle said.

Before she could answer, Lorenzo stepped out of his apartment. His face lit up when he saw Zoey.

"You're back!" he cried out.

"Well, that's a surprising change in attitude," Zoey said suspiciously. "Do I owe you money or something?"

"You're in with the Moretti Pack!" He hurried over to her, aglow with eagerness.

"No, I'm not." She shook her head decisively. "That's over. It's not happening."

"It's not?" A whiny note crept into his voice. "Can you call them back? Did you do something wrong? You can apologize, can't you? This could be my ticket in!"

Andrea burst out of her door wearing an apron, with flour on her hands. Stewart was right behind her. "Ticket into what, Lorenzo?" she demanded.

"Nothing." His face flushed and he glowered at the ground.

Andrea turned to Zoey. "So now you're recruiting children into gangs?" she said accusingly.

"Of course not!" Zoey said, appalled.

Andrea's eyes drilled into her. "My son was about to go back to school, and then that meeting happened where those horrible criminals killed Jordan. Lorenzo's been talking about that pack of animals nonstop. It's enough we paid protection money for nothing, but my son will *not* become a mobster."

"Jordan was ripping us off," Zoey corrected. "They addressed the problem the minute they found out about it. I mean, you can see the proof of it. They cleaned up the streets, they built that wonderful community garden."

"They are still extorting the local business owners out of

existence. They murder their enemies, and they kill anyone who crosses them. It's a dangerous and immoral lifestyle, and Lorenzo will have no part of it."

"Cut it out, Mom!" Lorenzo protested woefully. "Now she'll never introduce me to the *Capo*."

Andrea glared harshly at Zoey and grabbed Lorenzo's arm. Pausing, she flashed a despairing look at Stewart. "Today's not good for a coffee date, Stewart."

His face fell. "Well, that takes the cake, doesn't it?" He peered at her anxiously. "Get it, because you were making cake but now you're not?"

Andrea just looked at him blankly and dragged Lorenzo back into his apartment.

"She always laughs at my jokes," he muttered and wandered off, shoulders hunched.

"I did that," Zoey said, stricken. "That was all me. I ruined everything. I turned Lorenzo into a wanna-be thug, and I made Andrea hate me, and I ruined her and Stewart, and …" Her voice trailed off as she blinked back sudden tears. She loved to look on the bright side, but it was hard to see a bright side to ruining her friends' lives.

She waited for Danielle to say something crushing and sarcastic.

"It's okay," Danielle said weakly. "You didn't screw up too badly. Everything will be fine."

Wow. Things were pretty bad if Danielle was the optimistic one.

"Thanks. You're not the worst friend ever, no matter what anyone says," Zoey said.

Danielle laughed. "You pretty much *are*, but you're my only friend who's not super old like Andrea and Stewart, so I guess I'm stuck with you." Danielle wrinkled her brow. "Try not to die or anything, okay? I have a hard time making new friends. Lots of people say I'm bitchy and whiny."

"I don't believe that for a second. It implies some people actually don't think you're bitchy and whiny."

Danielle flicked Zoey on the head with her forefinger. "You're lucky I'm too tired to give you a beatdown for that comment. Well, tired and lazy."

"Right, I'll come back when you've got more energy and we'll duke it out," Zoey scoffed. "I gotta run. I'll see you around." She left the apartment, hopped on her bike, and headed back toward the east side.

Right away, she sensed an obstacle.

Frustration welled up inside her. She'd started checking the newspapers, and listening to the radio, and there was no reason for these obstacles. No car accidents, no rampaging creatures.

Obviously, they were specific to her, and she was getting fed up with it. Suddenly struck by inspiration, she pictured the obstacle as her destination so she could locate it. She circled around and dodged through back streets until she was able to sneak up behind it—or rather, her.

Watching the road Zoey would have taken, Giuliana sat in a van that was idling on a narrow side street.

Zoey hopped off her bike, stormed over to the van, and banged on the window. "Hey!" she bellowed. "You want me? Come and get me!"

Startled, Giuliana scrambled out of the van, slamming the door.

"You do know I'm a wolf, right?" She marched up to Zoey. "I can literally make you into sushi and eat you."

"I promise you'll suffer fatal indigestion." Zoey smiled at her unpleasantly. "And I'll rip off parts of your face you won't be able to grow back."

Giuliana glared at her. Apparently, she'd expected Zoey to be easily intimidated. She wouldn't be the first to assume the cheerful, funny, chubby girl would be easy to run over. Giuliana was about to find out she was very, very wrong.

Zoey had been bullied in grade school, until her parents took her to self-defense classes.

After that, her bullies started suffering a lot of bloody noses and loose teeth. Zoey had to spend plenty of afternoons in detention, but her parents had no problem with that whatsoever. While she couldn't win a fight against a wolf, she had been taught ways to leave permanent marks on them.

"How did you spot me?" Giuliana demanded.

"Magic in the blood. I have skills." Zoey folded her arms across her chest. "You keep stalking me, and now I'm here. Say your piece."

Giuliana drew herself up to her full height. "Fine. Stay the hell away from Dominic. Tell him you're not interested. Make him want to end it."

Seriously? All this grief because Giuliana was jealous?

"I have told him I'm not his mate. He's not listening. Something about his wolf choosing me on a full moon. You're a wolf; you should know what he's talking about." She shrugged. "Not much I can do about that."

"You don't seem to get it." Giuliana's eyes glowed a creepy yellow-orange. "Do whatever it takes to end it. You're not going to mate with him."

"That's not up to you, Giuliana."

"Isn't it?" Giuliana bared her fangs. "You're not good for him. End it, or I'll end you."

"You'll try."

Before Giuliana could say another word, Zoey lashed out with a quick foot sweep and knocked her on her butt. Hopping on her bike, she shot off through traffic, dodging expertly. Giuliana shifted and tried to chase her, but she was no match for the map witch. Zoey headed for the eastern side of town, the Bianchi Pack's territory. Surely, Giuliana wouldn't be stupid enough to chase her.

Except she was.

After about twenty blocks, Zoey heard screeching tires and a yelp.

Zoey pulled over on the sidewalk and craned her neck to see what had happened. Giuliana had been hit by a car, which was now speeding away. She was a block away from Zoey, crawling painfully to the sidewalk, still in wolf form.

Zoey leapt off her bike and ran over. Giuliana's leg was bent at a horrifying angle.

"Giuliana, oh my God! Are you all right?"

Giuliana's wolf lunged and snapped at her.

The hell with this.

Zoey wasn't going to die trying to help a pain-maddened, jealous she-bitch of a wolf. She grabbed her phone from her messenger bag.

Giuliana shifted back to human form in a flash. Standing naked on one leg, her face was white with pain. Zoey looked at her other leg, with the bone poking through the skin, and struggled not to barf.

"Who are you calling?" Giuliana cried out, panicked.

"I'm calling an ambulance, you moron! Your leg is broken!"

"Don't you dare!" Giuliana shouted. "Please," she choked out. "Don't call anyone. I have no right to ask you for a favor, but I'm asking."

Zoey was bewildered. "Why not? Is the pack abusing you? Are you afraid of them? I could help you find a place to hide. I've got map magic; I could take you somewhere really hard to find."

"Why would you?"

"Because it's what anyone would do."

Giuliana grimaced. "You'd be surprised."

"Giuliana, seriously. I'm ready to barf from just looking at your leg. I have to call the ambulance."

"I'm a healer!" Giuliana snapped. "I can heal myself. I don't want you to call anybody because if my uncle finds out I was chasing you, he'll lock me up in my room for a month. He's not abusive; it's just the way the pack works. He's an insanely overprotective ass." She looked positively pouty but not frightened.

Giuliana's leg began to straighten as Zoey watched. The flesh rippled and closed back over the bone, and the blood flow slowed.

"You're sure? Pack members aren't abusive?"

Giuliana gave her a sly look. "They're abusive to their mates. They beat them for the slightest offense."

"Wow, for someone who comes from a criminal organization, you really suck at lying." Zoey shook her head. "You actually want people to think that of your pack-mates?"

Giuliana's face contorted in frustration. "Fine. Our men don't beat their women; it goes against our pack's code. None of our women would tolerate it anyway. Doesn't matter. Stay the hell away from Dominic."

"Suddenly, I feel like calling him for a very romantic date. If you start following me again, I will not hesitate to snitch on you."

"You bitch!" Giuliana gasped.

"Thank you." Zoey gave a sarcastic curtsy. Climbing back on her bike, she peddled away, chased by a stream of what were probably very colorful insults in Italian. For all she knew, Giuliana could have been shouting the alphabet.

But she probably wasn't.

CHAPTER *Sixteen*

Dominic rained a hail of blows on the punching bag in the pack gymnasium at the back of the Arena. It exploded under the force, and he threw back his head and howled in fury. That was the third one this morning.

He was boiling with frustration. Zoey was nowhere to be found. Normally, he'd have men on her apartment twenty-four hours a day, but with the war against the Bianchi Pack, they didn't have the manpower. She'd briefly gone to her apartment yesterday, but by the time one of his men got there, she'd left again. Her friends claimed they had no idea where she was staying. He knew they were lying, but he also knew if he had them tortured to make them talk, she'd never speak to him again.

Damn, love was complicated.

His wolf was furious. It craved its mate, wanted to nuzzle her, smell her, press up against her. It wanted to feel the peace that came to him in her presence. Yesterday, he went running in the woods and challenged a bear to try to find some sort of release. The bear took one look at him, turned, and ran for its life.

After the night he'd spent with her, he couldn't believe she'd run off and leave him over one little argument.

It had been a hell of a week. The Bianchi Pack had burned down a restaurant under Moretti Pack protection. The Morettis were now rebuilding the restaurant and paying the owner for the loss of revenue. They'd kidnapped four Bianchi foot soldiers in revenge and blew up an armored truck carrying money from one of their casinos.

The Bianchis had refused to ransom their soldiers, who were still being held prisoner, so the Morettis dressed them in frilly outfits and sent pictures of them to taunt the Bianchis.

Dominic still hadn't been able to track down the business owners who'd gone missing. Arturo would only tolerate his failure for so long before doling out disciplinary action.

Romano had been trying to reach him all morning. Every time he answered, Dominic snapped, "Did you find her yet?" Romano's answer was always "no," and Dominic hung up on him.

As he swept up sand from the latest punching bag he'd destroyed, the door flew open, and Romano stalked in.

Dominic whirled to face him. "When did you decide life wasn't worth living?"

"There was an attack on one of our armored vans this morning," Romano said calmly. "The driver was badly burned. Arturo brought him here so Giuliana could heal him. Giuliana's pissed because she wasn't allowed to go to the scene and the driver nearly died. Arturo asked me to tell you since you're not answering your phone. He's on his way here. I told him you were already on it."

Dominic shook himself. "Fuck." Then he grimaced. "Thanks for covering for me." He dumped a dustpan full of sand into the trash.

"Always," Romano said promptly. "And no, we haven't located Zoey yet. She'll have to come up for air eventually. She has friends she cares about, and her bank account's running on fumes."

"All right. Damn, she's good at hiding." Dominic shook his head.

"Do you want my opinion?"

"Not ever, actually," he growled.

Romano bent down and scooped up some shreds of leather from the punching bag and tossed them into the trash. "You're letting the past hold you back. Zoey isn't … her." Wisely, he'd stopped himself from saying the name.

He knew what had happened to Dominic long ago and why he had gone wolf. But he had no right to bring that up.

"Tread very carefully."

Romano, as usual, ignored him. "You're letting a ghost get between you and the woman you moon-bit. And it's making you act like a real douche."

"Since when do you fucking care about the woman in my life?" Dominic snarled.

Romano's brows drew together, his eyes glowing in anger. "This isn't some roll in the hay. When it's a mate, that's different."

Dominic's wolf nearly exploded out of his skin. Instead, he took a swing at Romano, who just barely managed to duck. "If the next word out of your mouth involves Zoey, it will be your last."

Romano, in a rare moment of common sense, kept his lips zipped.

"And I am not driving her away," Dominic growled at him as he set the broom and dustpan in the corner. "I'm romancing her. I'm romancing the hell out of her."

"Damn. So sweet. Even I melted a little when you said that." Romano smirked and ducked to avoid Dominic's punch. "Too slow."

"You really have picked today as the day you want to die," Dominic said. "What do you want on your tombstone?"

"How about 'He died doing what he loved—annoying the shit out of people'. But really … now that you've moon-bit her, there's no going back, so you've got to make it work. You're buying her fancy things and nice dinners, but you're ignoring the one thing she's really asking for."

Dominic and his wolf began arguing. His wolf, pacing restlessly inside the cage of Dominic's humanity, wanted to be set free to tear off Romano's face. The human part of Dominic wanted to break down and ask Romano what that one thing was.

His phone started vibrating in the pocket of his jacket he'd hung on the wall. He grabbed it and answered.

"It's Zoey," he growled at Romano. "Take all your dumb advice and shove it up your ass."

"What did you say to me?" Zoey sounded shocked.

Carefully moving out of Dominic's reach, Romano threw back his head and howled with laughter.

"Not you!" Dominic shouted. "That wasn't for you! I was talking to a dead man. Where are you?"

"We're headed to the Arena. Are you there? Please be there."

The strain in her voice sent chills through him. "I'm here. I'll meet you out front." He broke into a trot. "What's wrong?"

"I'll tell you when I see you. We'll be there in five minutes," she replied, her voice frantic.

His hackles rose. Something had upset her. Why wouldn't she just let him keep her safe?

Romano was wheeze-laughing at getting Dominic in trouble with Zoey. Dominic, boiling with rage at whoever had hurt Zoey, swung around and punched Romano so hard, he heard ribs crunch. Romano fell over, still howling with laughter.

"Worth it!" he yelled after Dominic, and then got up and followed him, limping. His ribs would heal within the next few hours.

And what is Zoey asking for that I'm not giving her?

Dominic raced angrily down the hall. He gave her food and beautiful clothing and hot sex and himself, for the rest of his life. Wasn't that enough?

He knew he wasn't exactly experienced when it came to romance. Before Zoey, he'd had feelings for one woman. That woman was no longer in the picture because of Dominic. Because of his weakness.

He hadn't had to woo Phoebe, his high school sweetheart. He'd been human back then, and she'd sat next to him in English class. One day, she got busted passing him a note asking if he knew the answer to question 11 on their pop quiz. They'd spent the next week sitting next to each other in detention.

The rest was history.

Painful, heart-breaking history.

"All right, what?" he barked as Romano came limping up to him. "What does she really want from me, oh wise one?"

"She wants you to let her in. You're coming on all Big Bad Wolf telling her you're going to go kill a man, telling her she's going to be a mob wife, like it or not, and she's not allowed to ask any questions. No wonder she's hiding from you. If you stopped and explained things to her, you could turn it around."

Dominic gave him a look of disgust. *Let her in?* That was Romano's big idea? That had to be wrong. He was sorry he'd asked.

Maybe Giuliana could have given him a clue, but she got weird every time he even mentioned Zoey.

Minutes later, he stood on the sidewalk in front of the Arena as a taxi pulled up. Zoey spilled out of the cab, followed by a few friends of hers. There was Cin, the homeless thief. There was a frantic-looking middle-aged woman named Andrea, and Andrea's friend Stewart. They crowded around him, all babbling at the same time.

"What's going on?" he asked.

They all started answering at once.

"Quiet!" he bellowed. He pointed at Zoey. "You. What's happening?"

"Lorenzo's gone. Andrea's son." Zoey gulped a breath. She'd been crying. Whoever made her cry was going to swallow all of their teeth before they died. "The Bianchis took him."

"It's all your fault!" Andrea shouted and slapped Dominic across the face. She gasped and fell back a step.

He bared his fangs at the woman, who looked temporarily startled, but then she lunged at him and grabbed his shirt.

"My son is missing! They did it to get at you!" she shrieked.

He shook her off violently, but she was too frantic to be terrified. "Explain."

"My son started bragging about how he had a friend in the Moretti Pack. He's just a kid. He wants to be tough. He didn't mean anything by it." Andrea choked on a sob.

"And?"

"And he went to visit *her*, and she was hiding out in the Bianchi's territory …" She pointed at Cin furiously. Cin shriveled in on herself. "And they took him!" Andrea's face crumpled. "Save my son. Please! I'll give you everything I have."

Dominic shook his head impatiently. "I don't want your money. Where did they find him?" He glowered at Cin.

She started talking really fast. "We were dumpster diving at 37th and Fillmore. He saw a bunch of the Bianchi Pack members headed right for us, and he ran out to distract them so I could get away. I didn't want to leave him, I swear didn't, but he said if they grabbed both of us, nobody would know we'd been taken. He told me to find Zoey and get help."

Giuliana ran down the steps to join them. She glanced at Zoey but didn't say anything. Dominic quickly filled her in on what was happening.

"All right. Approaching them directly won't help," he said. "We can grab someone from the Bianchi Pack and put the screws to them and hope they know where he's been taken. We'll also have our *Strega* do a locate spell."

Andrea raised a brow. "What's a *Strega*?"

"A witch we contracted for the pack," Dominic replied. "Do you have anything of his? Some hair or an item of clothing?"

"No, I don't!" Andrea looked panicked. "God, I'm so stupid! I can go back home and get it, but that will take so long! They could be killing him!" She burst into loud sobs and collapsed in Stewart's arms.

"You can find the kid," Giuliana said to Zoey.

"Me? How?"

"You've got some kind of magic location powers, right?"

Dominic looked at Giuliana suspiciously. How did she know that? He hadn't told anybody.

"My powers? They're useless for this," Zoey protested. "I'm just a map witch. My power guides me through town and helps me avoid obstacles, but it doesn't find missing people. I'd do anything to find Lorenzo, but I can't."

"I've heard of map witches," Giuliana mused. "You can find any destination. Can't you imagine Lorenzo as your destination?"

"A person as my destination? I ..." Zoey looked at Andrea who was staring at her now, tear-stained eyes shining with hope. "I'll try." She closed her eyes and pictured Lorenzo. She imagined his narrow face topped by the mop of brown hair, his tall, skinny frame ... she pictured being in a car and driving toward him ... And she knew *exactly* where he was.

"East Main and 35th!" she cried out happily. "In the basement of an office building. Not only that, I can see the obstacles." She quickly described them to Dominic. Every obstacle was almost certainly a group of Bianchi shifter guards, and she knew how to steer him and his men around them.

"Call in the troops," Dominic said to Romano who took off at a dead run. He'd quickly round up the foot soldiers.

Dominic guided Zoey away from the rest of the group, a grim look on his face.

She put her hand on his arm, her brow crinkling with worry. "Be careful," she said. "And thank you so much. I hate to ask you to do something dangerous, but the Bianchis are going to make an example of Lorenzo to get at you guys, and he's just a naïve kid. I'd get him myself if I were capable."

"You've done your part. I would never let you go on a mission like that. Here's the deal, Zoey. If you want us to get your friend back, you agree to stay with me on pack property. You don't leave the property until the feud with the Bianchi Pack is settled."

She dropped her hand from his arm and took a step back.

"If I say no ... will you leave him there to die?" Acid dripped from every word.

"He's not one of us." It was what Arturo would have said without conscience or a second thought. It didn't make the words taste any better in his mouth.

Fury blazed in her eyes, but she gave a sharp, abrupt nod. "Fine," she snapped.

He'd been run over by a truck, shot, stabbed, set on fire, bitten by ghouls, punched by an ogre, and thrown off a fifty-foot cliff, but the look on Zoey's face caused him so much pain.

Dominic turned and hurried down the steps, praying he wouldn't be too late to save Lorenzo. If he was, it would break Zoey's heart.

CHAPTER SEVENTEEN

"Is that him?" Andrea jumped up from the overstuffed velvet chair and hurried to the window for the dozenth time that hour.

They were in the parlor of Arturo's house, a sprawling mansion on the outskirts of the northwest side of town. She looked out over the broad front lawn, her eyes laser-focused on every car that drove by. Arturo's property was ringed in by giant iron gates, which were adorned by enormous wolves and bristling with protective spells.

The car drove by the front gates.

"Not yet," she answered her own question, shoulders slumping in despair. She slunk back to the chair and collapsed.

Armed men and wolves paced the front of the property. Most of the pack members lived in houses scattered across the grounds. Wolves were social animals and needed to live together, or their animals risked going feral. The size and luxury of the pack members' homes depended on their position within the pack. The low-rank, single pack members lived in dormitory-style accommodations.

Cin sat hunched in her chair in the far corner of the room, hugging herself, steeped in misery. Stewart sat quietly in a chair next to Andrea's, looking wretched. Giuliana kept flipping the pages of a magazine she wasn't really reading.

"Andrea," Zoey said, "it's not Cin's fault. What did you want her to do, stay there and fight, all ninety-five pounds of her? Get killed or kidnapped? Did you want that skinny little girl to be in the hands of those Bianchi creeps?"

"No." Andrea scrubbed at her face with her hands. "Not that."

"Lorenzo's a big boy. He makes his own choices. Cin didn't hold a gun to his head and force him to visit her. And she's not a bad person. She takes care of a whole crew of homeless kids, keeps track of their whereabouts, and makes sure they have food and clean clothing and a place to sleep."

A small sound emanated from Cin. She was crying quietly. Andrea walked over to her and knelt next to her.

"I'm sorry," Cin said, her voice watery with tears. "I shouldn't have let him visit us. He isn't part of our world. I just liked him, you know? And when he talked about you, I'd pretend you were my mom too. But you aren't. I don't have a family. I don't deserve a family."

Andrea blinked hard and stared at Cin as if seeing her for the first time. "It's not your fault. Of course, you deserve a family," she said. "If your old family left you behind, they don't deserve *you*."

Cin cried harder, and Andrea pulled her into a hug.

"Hey, can I get in on that?"

Everyone looked up. Lorenzo stood in the doorway, battered and bruised, leaning on Dominic. Romano was right behind them. Lorenzo's eyes were blackened, nose swollen, and lips split, but he was alive. Cin shrieked with joy, Andrea burst into tears again, and everyone ran over to hug him. When they crowded around him, he cried out in pain. Giuliana elbowed them out of the way.

"Everyone back off!" she yelled. "Let me work my magic. Hugs can wait."

Lorenzo's knees gave way, and he fell into Dominic's arms. Romano scooped up Lorenzo and carried him off, and Giuliana walked with them, her hand on Lorenzo's arm. As long as she touched him, she could heal him. Andrea, Stewart, and Cin crowded around them as Romano headed to the clinic.

Dominic and Zoey were alone in the room now, standing a few feet apart. Zoey folded her arms defensively across her chest. Dominic had shed his suit jacket, and his white button-down shirt was splattered with blood. His movements were a little stiff, but he didn't seem to have any life-threatening injuries. Not for him, anyway.

"I am glad to see you made it back in one piece," she said frostily.

"That's what I do," Dominic said. "I live through things."

There was a weary, bitter tone to his words, along with a hint of haunted guilt. Zoey might have questioned it if she hadn't been simmering with fury.

"I'm having your stuff moved here, by the way," Dominic added.

"I see."

"And you're pissed at me."

She raked him with a furious scowl. "Using Lorenzo's life to blackmail me was a low, despicable move."

Dominic met her gaze, unblinking. "I did what needed to be done."

"Excuse me!" Ottavio's harsh tone made Zoey jump. He stalked through the door. Carlo bustled along behind him with his usual expression of dull, unfocused anger.

Ottavio fixed his icy gaze on Zoey. "I have been told you are now permanently living on pack property. Have you come to this house of your own free will?" he demanded.

Zoey returned his icy glower. "Yes, I have."

"And you know that, because of the wolf's bite, this may be your final month on this earth and you are not required to be here yet? You are granted that final month of freedom to say farewell to your loved ones if you so choose?"

Nice way to sugarcoat things.

"I am aware I am not required to be here."

Ottavio put his hand on her arm and led her across the room. Dominic watched, his eyes glowing with anger.

Ottavio leaned in and lowered his voice. "Did he coerce you? You didn't want to be here before, and now you do."

"I volunteered," Zoey said, shaking his hand from her arm. "Should you be touching me in front of my mate?" She flashed a poisonously sweet smile, and Ottavio's self-confident demeanor faded. He licked his lips nervously and glanced over at Dominic.

Dominic stalked across the room and maneuvered himself in between Zoey and Ottavio.

"No, he should not. He will not do it again. And I can hear every damn word you say, Ottavio. I may not be a born shifter, but I am a shifter nonetheless, and I've got shifter hearing. We're finished here."

Ottavio let out a threatening growl. "We're finished when I say we are." He returned his attention to Zoey. "You are a magic-blood. What are your powers?'

"None of your business." Dominic stepped between her and Ottavio. "She is my mate. She is here of her own free will. This conversation is over."

"It is absolutely my business. I need to know everything about her before I decide if she is permitted to stay here. Arturo's safety is my responsibility."

"He is *our* Alpha! It's the entire pack's responsibility! Do you imply his safety is not my first priority?" Dominic's ears went pointy and furry, and dark claws shot from his fingertips.

Ottavio's lip wrinkled in a snarl. "I imply nothing. I openly state you have been making many questionable decisions which weaken the pack." He looked at Zoey as he spoke and twisted his lips into an ugly snarl. "We can take it outside."

"Gladly." Dominic's eyes glowed.

"Enough!" A wave of power rolled into the room, making Zoey's hair frizz. She felt as if she'd rolled in static electricity.

Arturo strolled in, big and imposing. His cold blue gaze swept the room, and he looked Zoey up and down slowly. "Welcome to our house." He glanced at Ottavio. "Biting Zoey was a decision Dominic's wolf made. I do not expect to hear you bring it up again. As for her staying here, I can sense her powers. She is an Earth witch of low-level magic abilities. She is no danger to me, and my herb garden will enjoy the benefits." His lips quirked in a brief smile. Then he gestured at Ottavio and Carlo. "Come with me. I require your assistance."

Ottavio and Carlo followed him out of the room, shooting dirty looks over their shoulders.

Zoey waited until they were gone before she spoke to Dominic. "I said I'd stay under this roof. I didn't say I'd stay with *you*. I would like my belongings moved into my own room."

Dominic's expression turned bleak, but he nodded. "As you

wish."

CHAPTER EIGHTEEN

The gardens surrounding Arturo's mansion were a patchwork of miracles.

Some of the land was xeriscaped with cactus and other succulents, stone arrangements, and statues of wolves. However, there were enormous sections of lush, tropical landscape with a cluster of rain clouds hanging over them. It only rained at night, and it always rained just the right amount. Arturo would have needed a full-time upper-level weather witch on hand to maintain that, which would be ungodly expensive. There were citrus fruit trees and pomegranate trees and pineapple trees. Waterfalls gushed into crystal ponds.

Arturo had "requested" Zoey's friends stay as guests in his mansion for the time being because he didn't want the Bianchis to be able to use them as collateral again. Nobody turned down Arturo's "requests," so there they all were. Danielle, Zoey, Andrea, Cin, and Stewart had just finished a late afternoon snack of coffee and biscotti served to them in a gazebo.

At the moment, though, Andrea was blind to the beauty surrounding them. Her attention was focused on Lorenzo, who was leaning on his crutches and talking to Dominic.

He'd suffered shattered ribs, a fractured arm, and broken nose and cheekbones at the hands of the Bianchis, and he was still recuperating. Giuliana's healing powers had saved him weeks of healing time, but he was only human.

Cin was in a funk too.

She'd confided her woes in Zoey. Lorenzo used to hang on her every word, and now all his attention seemed to be laser-focused on the Moretti *Capo*. She was happy Arturo had relocated the rest of her homeless friends back to the Moretti territory, moving them into a motel where they were provided with hot showers and food. He'd even given them all jobs—painting over the vacant buildings they'd spray-painted. But she apparently hadn't realized how much she'd taken Lorenzo's feelings for her for granted—until he started ignoring her.

Zoey had no idea what Dominic and Lorenzo were talking about, and she wasn't about to ask him. She'd spent the last three days treating Dominic as if he were a troll with full-body herpes. She couldn't get past the fact Dominic would have let an innocent teenager die if she'd refused to stay with him. Dominic didn't deserve Lorenzo's hero worship, but telling Lorenzo would have been pointless.

"I've lost him," Andrea said miserably. "How can I compete against a Moretti *Capo*? He'll join the pack and get himself killed."

"I wouldn't worry about that. Lorenzo's not Moretti material," Zoey said, then winced. That hadn't come out right. "I'm not trying to be mean. I'm just saying he isn't physically big enough that anyone would allow him to be bitten by a warrior-class shifter. He would never survive the turn."

"They must want my son for something. Why else would Dominic have been talking to him?" Andrea wiped tears from her cheeks. "They'll use him as cannon fodder."

Andrea had to be right. Dominic didn't do anything unless he had something to gain.

"If they do that, I'll never talk to Dominic again," Zoey said, eyes blazing.

"But my son would be dead." Andrea's voice was flat and hopeless. Lorenzo's head was tipped up, riveted by whatever Dominic was saying, his head bobbing with eagerness. "I'm going to my room. I can't watch."

"I'll go too," Stewart said, standing with a sigh. "I've got a chair to finish."

Arturo had provided Stewart with woodworking tools, and he'd even commissioned multiple pieces of hand-carved furniture from Stewart. Under other circumstances, Stewart would have been over the moon, but Andrea's misery weighed like a dark heavy cloud on everyone. They were all worried about Lorenzo, who was young and impressionable and so desperate for a father figure, he'd make poor decisions.

"Yeah, me too," Cin sighed. "I'm going to go work on some jewelry."

"About that," Zoey said. "I never apologized for thinking you'd shoplifted the jewelry. I'm really sorry." She was wearing a bracelet that Cin had made for her.

Cin managed a wry smile. "Why would you think anything else of me?"

"Cin, you've got to value yourself more than that. You should have told me off, and I would have deserved it."

"It's no big deal."

After Cin left, Zoey nudged Danielle with her elbow. "Go on. Your turn to complain. Everyone else is miserable."

Danielle stood. "Nah. Arturo's chef, Tony, taught me how he makes coffee. In case you haven't noticed, this particular variety is the nectar of the gods. I'm actually in a good mood for the moment."

"The hell you say?" Zoey bugged her eyes wide open in fake astonishment.

"God's honest truth. Now, when I leave here and no longer have access to the imported coffee beans and the bomb-ass coffee maker, you can expect to hear weeping and wailing from morning to night. You've been warned."

"When you talk about the bomb-ass coffee maker, are you referring to Tony, or the equipment?" Zoey pinned her friend with a questioning gaze.

"Shut up, that's what. I need more coffee, and Tony promised he'd teach me his mother's secret recipe for espresso. Oh damn, I've said too much. I'm leaving, I'm leaving!" Danielle got up and ran out of the room.

Zoey began wandering the grounds, instinctively drawn to drooping flowers and plants. They perked up as she trailed her fingers over them. Yay. At least she was able to make *something* feel better today.

A patter of footsteps crunching on gravel made her spin around defensively. Giuliana was coming her way. As ever, she was dripping in Versace and Prada, and her pretty face was pinched in a scowl.

"Oh, hold on." Zoey reached into her pocket and pulled out a canister of pepper spray. She smiled at Giuliana without warmth. "Now we're good."

"That was hilarious. So funny. I nearly died," Giuliana said flatly.

Zoey turned down a side path and kept walking. Giuliana caught up with her.

"Thank you for not telling on me," she said grudgingly.

"Whatever." Zoey shrugged. She wasn't going to tattle on Giuliana, but she also hadn't forgotten Giuliana's attempts to bully and threaten her.

She walked faster, but Giuliana easily kept pace.

Zoey shot her an annoyed look. "We both know you don't like me, so this isn't a social visit. What do you want?"

"You're ignoring Dominic.," Giuliana said, sounding aggrieved. "It's been three days. His wolf is going crazy."

"Huh. I remember some crazy she-bitch stalking me and threatening me to stay away from Dominic. Oh wait, that was you," Zoey said. "And now you're pushing me toward him? I thought you wanted him for yourself."

"You thought *I* wanted him?" Giuliana's face scrunched in horror. "Ew. He's super old. He's like thirty-five or something. I mean, not as bad as the other people my uncle was thinking of pawning me off to, but still, definitely not my dream wolf. I threw myself a little party when I found out I didn't have to be his mate."

Zoey stopped walking and stared at her, baffled. "Then what was your problem with him choosing me as a mate?"

"I thought you bewitched him or something."

"You thought I bewitched him? Why? How?"

Giuliana lifted her narrow shoulder in an uneasy shrug. "You have magic. I can smell it on you. Some kind of witch's charm. And lots of women would give their right tit to be a *Capo*'s mate."

"But his wolf moon-bit me."

Giuliana looked away. "Yeah. I guess I didn't believe it was real."

"Why not?" Zoey said indignantly.

Giuliana shrugged. "No reason."

"Because … this?" Zoey gestured at herself.

"Because you're … wearing polka dots?" Giuliana cast a critical eye on Zoey's blouse. "I mean, not a fashion choice I personally would have made. I wouldn't even call it a fashion choice, actually—"

"No, dork-face, because I'm fat."

"What does that have to do with anything?" Giuliana sounded as if she were genuinely baffled. "You're full-figured. You're cute enough. I mean, you're not my type, but I don't swing that way. I see guys here checking you out … very carefully so Dominic doesn't catch them doing it and kill them, but still, they look. So men must find you hot."

"Thank you? Or screw you? I'm not sure which." Zoey started walking again. "But you're still not answering my question. Why did you warn me away from him if you don't want him for yourself? Why do you care what happens with him?"

"Because he's my friend, and he's also genuinely a good person," Giuliana said heatedly. "He deserves a mate who loves him and is devoted to him, and I'm still not sure if that's you. He's got a good heart, through and through. Out of all the people in the Moretti Pack, he's the one I trust the most."

"Dominic?"

Giuliana glared at her. "See, there you go. Judging him when you don't know a thing about him."

Zoey felt like a boiling over tea kettle. "Because he won't *tell* me a damn thing! I know he kills people without question when his boss tells him to. I know he's ordered me to be his mate but tells me I don't get to know a damn thing about pack business, and he expects me to just deal with it. He's got mile-high walls, and when I try to get him to open up the least little bit, he acts like a complete ass."

Giuliana's face turned red and she clenched her fists. "He is loyal, he's protective, he's self-sacrificing. And if you don't appreciate that, you really don't deserve him!" she shouted before turning on her heel and storming off.

Zoey stalked after her and grabbed her shoulder, and Giuliana spun on her with a snarl, her mouth filled with fangs.

"You know, for someone who wants people to treat her like a

grownup, and who doesn't want to be seen as riding on her uncle's coattails, you really act like a tantruming little brat."

Giuliana's eyes flew open with shock. "What did you just say to me? *Do you know who I am?*" Giuliana's fangs shot from her gums, and her words ended on a snarl.

Zoey fixed Giuliana with a scornful gaze. "Yes, and I know who your uncle is. Going to run and tell? Is that how you handle things?"

Giuliana glared daggers at Zoey. Sucking in a breath, she let it out very slowly. "No."

"If you grow up a little and learn to talk to people without threatening, screaming, and then stomping off, people might start to take you seriously."

Zoey left Giuliana standing there with her mouth hanging open.

Zoey headed back to the house, and as she made her way through the garden, she spotted Dominic. It had been really, really hard to stay away from him. She missed seeing him light up when she walked in the room. She missed his smile and the way his gaze warmed her. She missed their back-and-forth sparring. She missed giving him a hard time—both literally and figuratively. She felt pretty and funny and all-around good when she was with him. *He* made her feel that way.

When he saw her looking at him, he waved. She sighed and waved back, gesturing at him to come over.

He instantly stood and hurried toward her, which she grudgingly had to admit was pretty flattering.

"Um, hello," she said. "So, oddly enough, Giuliana claims you're actually a nice person."

"She did?" Dominic pretended to look appalled. "Remind me to give her a beat-down later."

"You don't always have to put on the tough guy act."

"It cuts me to the quick that you think it's an act," Dominic smirked.

"Ah ha! We're getting somewhere. I cut you to the quick? I didn't even think you had a quick. So you *do* have feelings."

He grinned. "Only for you, princess."

Zoey rolled her eyes. "Say something real, Dominic."

"You look lovely today. When I woke up, I wanted to find you in my arms."

"That's flattery and flirtation. It's not real." She started to walk away.

"Wait!" Dominic said with genuine urgency in his voice.

Zoey stopped and turned around. Dominic surveyed the area, as if making sure nobody was watching, and then dropped to one knee in front of her.

Then he started singing. The Italian words rolled out, lush and deep. His voice was astounding, so smooth and self-assured.

She couldn't understand a word of the song, so she just closed her eyes and let the melody flow over her. It soaked into her, stroking the depths of her soul.

When he stopped, she waited a moment or two before opening her eyes.

"Your voice is very good," she said.

He climbed to his feet again, brushing his knees off and looking abashed.

"Yep, surprised me too."

"It did? You don't normally sing?"

"Not since I was a little boy, when I was in the church choir."

"What do the words mean? Is this something you sang in church?"

"It's an old Italian love song." He frowned. "My father used to sing it to my mother. But I'd rather not talk about my parents right now."

"If you don't normally sing, why did you do it just now?"

He cleared his throat. "Don't laugh."

There was a vulnerable, boyish quality to him now, and she knew it was just for her. She'd asked himself to open himself up, and he had—as much as he was capable. For a man like him, that had to be hard. And he was making the effort for her.

She shook her head solemnly. "I promise I won't."

"Lorenzo said women like it when you sing to them."

"You took love advice from a seventeen-year-old?"

He winced. "Seventeen and eleven months and one week. A grownup, really."

"That's what you were talking to him about? His mother and I thought you were trying to sell him on being a Moretti foot soldier."

Dominic barked out a laugh. "I've been doing anything but. He'd join our pack yesterday if I let him. I told him the pack would give him a scholarship and put him through school, and if he graduates from college with a degree in computer science, he could work for one of our businesses managing computer security."

"Oh," Zoey said, taken aback. She hadn't expected that from Dominic. "How did he respond?"

"Disappointed at first, but he cheered up at the thought he could be associated with us on any level."

"But again," she squinted up at him. "you took love advice from Lorenzo?"

"Well, nothing else seemed to be working."

She shook her head in frustration. "What did you expect? Did you not realize that blackmailing me into staying here by threatening to let Lorenzo *die* would make me very, very angry?"

"Yes," he agreed. "But I would have done whatever it took to get you to agree to let me protect you. I'd rather have you hate me and be safe than be happy with me but in danger."

"Oh," she said quietly. She hadn't considered it from that angle. How had he managed to make being a total asshole sound sweet? "You know, if you'd just take the time to explain things to me, we might get on a lot better."

"Romano told me that too. Dammit, I hate when that hairy bastard is right." Dominic made a sour face. "It's not personal, I promise you. I've just lived my life a certain way for the last ten years. I've built up walls so thick, no light could get through. Until you came along." His blue eyes shone with warmth. He was focused on her, as if nothing else existed. "You're my light, Zoey. You're finding the cracks in my armor."

"Oh," Zoey said in wonder and blinked back hot tears. Nobody else had made her feel like this. And, she realized, nobody ever would. This connection between them was special and unique. And he needed her help. Without her, those walls would stay up around his heart and he'd never let himself feel all the things he deserved to feel. Being loved, being cherished. "That's amazing."

"If I agree to try harder from now on, would you consider going out to dinner with me tonight?"

"Well ..." she pretended to consider for a moment. He looked at her expectantly, clearing his throat. "You *did* sing to me."

"Yes, I did!" Dominic gave her a winning smile. "And very well, too, if I do say so myself."

"If you can get Lorenzo to apologize to his mother for being an ass and reassure her he's not going out on shoot-em-up missions with your pack, I will gladly have dinner with you."

He lit up. "I will do better than that. Fetch Andrea and come meet me in the parlor in fifteen minutes."

A short while later, Dominic led a shame-faced Lorenzo into the parlor. Andrea, Stewart, and Zoey were waiting.

"Tell your mother why you wanted to join our pack," Dominic said in a stern voice.

"It's the best way I could think of to keep you safe!" Lorenzo flushed, shoving his hands in his pockets. "You gave up everything to move here with me, and we live right next to the portal, one of the most dangerous places in the city. On my own, I can't do anything to protect you. But if I was a member of the Moretti Pack, I'd make enough money that we could live somewhere safer, and nobody would dare mess with my family. And yeah, I wanted to help out Cin too. I thought if we had a bigger place I could," his cheeks glowed red, "ask her and her friends to live with us or something."

Andrea burst into happy tears and hugged her son.

Cin, who had walked into the room unnoticed, said in a small voice, "You'd let someone like me live in your house?"

"We would," Andrea said with motherly warmth, and then Cin joined the hug, followed by Stewart.

Lorenzo stepped back and looked at Stewart. "You make my mom happy. You tell really, really stupid jokes, but my mom thinks they're funny. I guess 'cause she's old like you. If the two of you went out on a," he made a horrible face, "date, I guess it wouldn't be the end of the world. Just don't tell me anything about it."

Stewart began to cry and hugged Andrea, and Andrea hugged her son. Zoey blinked her eyes and wiped at them with the back of her hand.

"Shut up. I'm not crying, you're crying," she sniffled to Dominic. "I need to go find a dress for dinner tonight."

"I have a closet full of evening gowns for you in our bedroom." At her surprised expression, Dominic winked with a very smug look on his face. "I knew you'd come around sooner or later. I thought it would be sooner, honestly. I'm pretty damn charming, after all."

"Oh my God, are you insufferable." But she smiled as she followed him out of the main house, across the grounds, and over to a very nice Mediterranean-style three bedroom with red barrel tile roofs.

CHAPTER *Nineteen*

"Before you get ready for dinner, we need to talk." Dominic backed Zoey up against the velvet wallpaper of his bedroom's far wall.

"About what?"

"About the fact I'm not going to be able to wait until after dinner."

"Are you going to make me regret coming in here with you?"

"Definitely." He grabbed her hands and pinned them above her head. "You made me wait. You drove my wolf crazy. You were so close, but you weren't with me. I've been sleeping alone when I should have been sleeping with my mate."

"Your mate? As in me?"

"Of course, you numbskull. Sexy numbskull," Dominic added hastily.

"Just checking."

He lowered his head and nipped her neck hard enough to make her yelp, but there was a hot pleasure in it too. "You want to know about wolves and mating? Let me start educating you."

"Ooh. Suddenly, I'm hot for teacher." Wow, she'd never been so bold before.

Dominic slid his other hand down her back, and Zoey arched toward him. He took an appreciative whiff and curved his hand around her belly. For the first time, she didn't have the slightest urge to suck it in.

His sexy voice zinged through her body, blasting away any self-consciousness, and somehow her panties magically disappeared. Oh, wait, what were her hands doing? Her bra joined her panties. Zoey was naked, one raw conduit of need. Both his hands were now cupping her generous backside, kneading the flesh of her cheeks.

She fought the urge to climb onto him.

He picked her up effortlessly, as if she weighed nothing. She had never felt so desired before.

Carrying her over to the massive bed, Dominic sat on the edge of the mattress with her in his arms. She was boneless with want, her skin against the wool of his suit, the breadth of his chest.

He lowered her carefully, as if she were a work of art, and stroked her breasts, stomach, the sides of her thighs—everywhere but her damp girly bits—with his broad palms. It drove her crazy with desire, and she squirmed, biting back a whimper at his sweet torture.

Finally, he slid one hand between her legs and lightly ran his fingertips over the seam of her pussy. Her breath hitched, her legs parting wider in invitation.

Dominic dragged his fingers through her dampness, and her legs trembled. Then his hand vanished as he began stripping off his clothing.

"Faster," she urged, which just made him slow down. Her gaze was riveted on him as he slowly peeled off his jacket.

"How are you doing, Zoey Monroe?"

"Very, very good," she smiled.

"It'll get better," he assured her.

He slid a finger between her legs, and she shivered violently.

"More showing and less telling, Mr. Modest."

"Hmmph. There's nothing modest about me." He pretended to be offended, but the proof was in the hard ridge pressing against Zoey's side.

She shrieked as he flipped her over and bent her over the bed, her face pressed against the mattress. He was on his feet behind her, with his palms on her sides. He trailed his fingers lightly along her curvy body.

"All this woman, all mine. How did I get so lucky?"

He squeezed her butt cheeks with his massive palms. She shivered at the sensation of his fingers on her lit nerve endings. She shifted her weight, leaning into his touch, before he slipped one hand between the folds of her pussy, slick with her excitement. He touched her clit, and she jolted as if she had come in contact with a live wire.

A moan escaped as his fingers did delicious, swirly things that drove her wild. And then … he removed his hand.

What?

"Don't even *think* of stopping now, you bastard!"

He let out low, sexy rumble of laughter.

"Dammit, Dominic, if you don't take me right now—*oh!*"

She gasped as he slammed his enormous length into her from behind, filling her.

His hand returned to do its delirium-inducing thrumming against her clit as he rolled his hips over and over against her backside.

She clutched at the bedspread, thick waves of unruly brown hair fanning about her head, muffling the moans and sighs as he rocked her body with each thrust.

His fingers continued their hypnotic strokes, and together their breaths grew harsher and faster, almost in unison as they both began the climb toward the apex of pleasure. The heat coiled deep inside her until she shattered with a loud cry.

Waves of ecstasy pulsed through her, and her walls squeezed his thickness. He answered her cry with a loud, animalistic growl and shuddered with his release. She felt his hot seed filling her and gloried in knowing she'd given him so much pleasure.

He stayed inside her until the waves finally succeeded. When he slid out, he pulled her back up from the bed, taking her into his arms.

He looked at her face with a warmth that wrapped her like a blanket and seeped into her soul.

"I love you," he said, caressing her cheek with his thumb. "I need you. Every day that goes by without you by my side is dull and colorless. If you'll just stay with me, I'll be a better mate to you. I swear on the honor of the pack."

**

Dominic walked to the back door of the limo and held it open for Zoey. She couldn't help but feel a rush of warmth. The big, scary killer was also an old-fashioned gentleman. And he treated her like a princess.

He was a complicated man made up of many parts. Sure, some of them were sharp and spikey, but now that she'd gotten to know him, she understood those were barriers he'd erected to protect himself.

"Hey!" a voice shouted from behind a cluster of palm trees. Romano trotted up, looking expectant. "What's up, boss?"

"Going to dinner."

Romano's face lit up. "Nice. I'm hungry. Where are we going? I'm in the mood for a rare steak."

"We, as in *my mate and I,* are going to Sergio's. You are going to sit outside and eat a sandwich."

Romano frowned and slumped his shoulders. "Sergio's? I love Sergio's."

"We'll bring you leftovers," Zoey promised him, elbowing Dominic.

Romano looked at them with sudden interest. "Wait, are you guys going on an actual date? Did Dominic stop acting like an ass?" He sniffed the air. "What is that smell? Did you make the beast with two backs? Ha, get it? Because he's a beast and— Awwwk!" He struggled to breathe, which was hard to do with Dominic crushing his windpipe.

"Dominic, please don't break your friend," Zoey said, sliding into the back seat of the car. "You might regret it later."

"Doubtful," he grunted but released his hold on Romano's neck.

Romano coughed and wheezed dramatically from the front seat as their limo driver headed to Sergio's until Dominic kicked the back of his seat and he stopped.

"You guys are like brothers who fight all the time," Zoey laughed.

"He's adopted," Dominic said promptly. "His real mother was a troll."

It was about a half-hour drive, but traffic was light, and Zoey sank into a warm haze of contentment. Dominic's massive arm wrapped around her shoulders, and she leaned against him in companionable silence. This felt good. This felt right. Like she was exactly where she was supposed to be.

Suddenly, a blinding sense of panic choked Zoey. "Obstacle. Turn back!"

"You heard her!" Dominic yelled. He wrapped his arms around Zoey protectively as the driver tried to make a quick turn in the middle of the street.

A massive explosion rattled the air, and everything went dark.

CHAPTER TWENTY

Dominic's ears rang, and his mouth tasted like blood. He tried to shake Giuliana's hand off of him, and she tightened her grip on his wrist.

"Hold still so I can heal you, you ass!" Giuliana barked.

"I'm healed enough!" Dominic groaned and stumbled to his feet. "We've got to find her. And you need to go back home."

He was in the middle of a scene that echoed a long-ago nightmare. Did the Bianchi Pack know what had happened to him all those years ago? Was that why they'd attacked him when he was with his mate?

When he was human, there had been an ogre attack. He and his fiancée, Phoebe, had been enjoying lunch together when the screaming started. Dozens of rage-filled ogres barreled down the street. Bodies flew through the air, and cars were overturned.

He'd grabbed her, and they'd run. He pushed her ahead of him, and then the trolls closed in, and he'd tried to put his body between hers and theirs.

As a human, he was no match for them. They'd snatched her away, just as the police arrived—too late.

And now, he'd failed the woman he loved—again. Despite being bitten, training as a foot soldier, and working his way up through the ranks, Dominic still couldn't protect those he loved.

The twisted wreck of the limo stretched sideways in the middle of the street. The scene was crawling with cops, but they were very careful to stay out of Dominic's way. Most of the cops were on the Moretti Pack payroll.

The explosion had sent their car spinning, and the door had been ripped from its hinges. Their driver was dead. When Dominic lunged from the car, he'd been stunned by a hail of silver bullets. They couldn't kill a warrior-class shifter, but they'd knocked him out, and he'd sprawled on the ground, fading in and out of consciousness, until Giuliana showed up.

Dante was healing Romano.

Other pack members were on the scene too, some in wolf form, sniffing around. Unfortunately, Zoey had been pulled into a van, and Dominic's scenters had no idea where the van was.

Right before he'd passed out, Dominic had called headquarters, and they'd been able to seal off the roads bordering their territory. The van had tried to cross back over to the east side, but they'd run into a roadblock and driven off.

The van had vanished though. It could be anywhere.

And now more bad news was storming up in the form of Arturo, with Ottavio and Carlo on his heels.

Giuliana stepped away from Dominic, folding her arms defensively in front of her face.

"What the hell is my niece doing out here at the scene of an attack?" Arturo bellowed. The bones on his face rippled, and his ears were pointy and fur tipped.

"I came without asking him. He was semi-conscious when I got here and started healing him. The minute he gained consciousness, he tried to push me away and send me home." Giuliana was pale, her voice weak.

"You'd say anything to cover for Dominic," Ottavio snapped at her.

"Bite me, asshole," she spat at him. "You'd say anything to get another *Capo* in trouble."

"You are coming home," Arturo growled at her, "and you will not leave the house without a squad of bodyguards. Ever again."

Giuliana's face went white with anger. "You will regret this," she informed her uncle. Her back was stiff with fury as she let two foot soldiers escort her to an SUV.

Arturo spun on Dominic with a snarl. "And you! Letting her come here? It's only the fact I owe you my life many times over that keeps you breathing. You are no longer a *Capo*. You are no longer in my pack."

Dominic stared at him in shock and swallowed hard. Just like that. His pack, his family, his protection, his identity—snatched away from him.

"Yes, sir," he said tonelessly.

That meant he was searching for Zoey on his own.

"I respectfully request release from the pack, to go with Dominic," Romano said.

"I don't want you," Dominic bit out. "You're no good to me. You never have been. You do nothing but get in my way, and I'm sick of carrying your deadbeat ass. As soon as I claim my mate, I will be leaving the city, and I will not be taking you with me." He saw the look of dark hurt in Romano's eyes. Life outside the pack would be too dangerous. And the only way to get rid of the big, loyal bastard was to make him hate Dominic.

Romano's face went blank.

Dominic turned and walked away quickly. He made it around the block before he shifted, threw back his head, and howled in rage.

Thoughts of Zoey floated in his head. *She needs me.* He couldn't go feral and give up now. With agonizing effort, he grabbed hold of his wolf and wrestled it back inside him. His wolf didn't want to go, and it fought him all the way, making the transition sheer torture. He broke his bones to force them back into human shape and dragged his fur back under his skin.

He couldn't think as well when he was a wolf. He needed to be able to plan, to strategize.

He crouched on the ground, panting.

Think, stupid bastard, think! Was Arturo going to cancel the blockade and let the van with Zoey escape? No, he probably wouldn't do that because the van full of Bianchi wolves had invaded Moretti territory, and Arturo needed to capture and kill them.

If Dominic was no longer a Moretti, then Zoey was no longer Arturo's concern. Zoey thought Dominic was hard-hearted and calculating—Arturo made Dominic look like a girl scout.

A familiar voice sliced through his fog of panic. Romano came barreling toward him, furious.

"Fuck! I've lost her, dammit!" Dominic howled his sorrow. "Go away, Romano! I can't save you. I can't save anyone!"

"I never asked you to save me, asshole!" Romano barked at him. "I asked you to let me serve by your side, and that's where I am as long as I'm breathing."

Dominic fixed his bleary gaze on Romano. "I don't deserve you. And I have to go look for Zoey now."

"Cin just called me. She's got a line on where they are. Street kid network; they all keep in touch with each other. 37th and Harris. And no, you don't deserve me, but you're fucking stuck with me."

He was talking to Dominic's backside because the second Romano said the street names, Dominic had gone wolf again and tore down the street.

**

"Are we there yet?" Zoey chanted as they drove. "Are we there yet? Are we there yet?"

"Shut up!" Luigi, Primo's nephew, bellowed in frustration. "Dammit," he complained to Salvatore, Primo's first in command. "Just let me kill her!"

Salvatore shook his head. "Your uncle said no. She's more useful alive. For now."

Luigi's lip wrinkled in a snarl. "Doesn't mean I can't slap you around some," he growled. "Say 'are we there yet' one more time. I dare you!"

Zoey grinned, her eyes glowing with malice. "Are we there yet? Are we—"

Luigi's fist shot toward her face. Salvatore was faster and grabbed his wrist. "Your uncle said no! If you hit her too hard, she'll die!"

"So what?" Luigi yelled. "Nobody disrespects me like that! Let the fuck go of me!"

He struggled, and Salvatore held his wrist. Luigi and Salvatore fell to the floor in the back of the van, wrestling with each other. Zoey took the opportunity to jump to her feet, lunged for the back door of the van, and fumbled for the lock.

Before Salvatore and Luigi could grab her, the door flew open and she fell out onto the street. The van was only moving at a crawl because they were cruising around the west side, trying to find a way to get past Arturo's men. They'd been complaining about it the whole time.

They were on a tiny side street. Zoey shot down the street, heart in her throat, and made it to the main road, but a growl behind her made her spin around. She stared at two large, angry wolves. Salvatore and Luigi faced her with their tails swishing.

There was no point in running, but she wouldn't make this easy for them.

"You fleabags are going to have to drag me back," she yelled. "I'll gouge your eyes out, you mangy poodles!"

They froze, turned, and ran.

Wow. Was she a badass and had never known it?

"Yeah, you'd better run!" she yelled at their retreating backs.

Then she saw what they were running from: two more enormous wolves were barreling down the street toward her. Dominic and Romano.

They reached her and shifted back to human form. Dominic grabbed her and squeezed her so tightly, she groaned in protest.

Zoey looked up at him, blinking away tears of relief, love, and gratitude. "What took you so long?"

CHAPTER *TWENTY-ONE*

Before they went into Dominic's apartment above the restaurant, Romano tromped up the stairs to make sure it was safe. Then he went back downstairs and gestured at them to go inside.

"We're here instead of Arturo's?" Zoey said, flopping onto Dominic's couch. "I mean, I'm certainly happy to be closer to Sergio's restaurant, but wouldn't it be safer at Arturo's right now?"

"Romano, wait in the hall," Dominic said.

Romano obeyed instantly, leaving the apartment and closing the door behind him. Dominic sank down onto the pillow next to Zoey, his eyes hollow and his face grim.

"What's wrong?" Zoey had never seen Dominic look so ... lost.

"Nothing's safe right now, Zoey," Dominic said grimly. "Arturo believes I put his niece in danger, and therefore, he has kicked me out of the pack. As a lone wolf, I can't offer you the same kind of protection I would have before. If you want me to relinquish my claim—"

"What did you just say to me?" Zoey spluttered. "That's ... I don't ... I'm seriously tempted to punch you right now. The only reason I don't is because it would hurt me more than it would hurt you."

"You're not relieved to be rid of me?"

Zoey thought she might explode, she was so furious. "You win first prize for being the dumbest wolf on the face of God's green earth. Abandoning a mate claim ... your wolf would be okay with that?"

He shook his head in resignation. "No. My wolf would go crazy. And it would take me with it."

"And you didn't think that was information you should share with me?" she yelled and punched his arm. "Ow! And now you hurt my hand!"

"I would do anything to keep you safe. I would die for you. And that's why I'm willing to set you free. Right now, I'm a lone wolf caught in the middle of a pack war, and you're my mate, which paints a big fat target on your back."

"You're not lone; you still have me!" Romano called from the hallway.

"*Stop listening!*" Dominic growled. "Good God. Can't a man do something heroic and self-sacrificing without an audience?"

"How about cowardly and insulting?" Zoey said angrily. "How could you think so little of me that I'd abandon you at the first sign of danger? And how dare you give up on yourself like that?"

"I knew she was a keeper!" Romano yelled.

Dominic leapt to his feet. "*I will kill you*," he shouted at the door so loudly, the walls shook and a painting fell to the floor.

"I'm going to wait downstairs so you can guys can not-have sex!" Romano shouted back, and they heard his footsteps pounding down the stairway.

Dominic sat down again.

"I will consider being your mate," Zoey said, struggling to contain her hurt and fury, "on one condition. *You stop hiding things from me.* Right now, you're treating me like a bed partner, not a real mate or wife, and I will not accept that. I deserve better than that." She blinked away tears. "You've made me feel like I deserve better, but every time I start to get close to you, you do something to push me away. Don't try to deny it."

Dominic chewed his lip, anguish sparking in his eyes. "You're right. Romano was right too, which I am never going to live down, but most importantly, you're right. And I am so very, very sorry. You do deserve better from me."

"Then tell me why you shut me out."

"Because everyone I've ever loved has died," he said bleakly. "And I'm afraid I can't keep you safe."

His pain settled around her like a damp, chill cloud. "Who did you love?"

"My parents. I was ten. My father was low-level mafia, human mafia, and my mother was collateral damage when their car exploded. I was sent to live with an aunt and uncle, along with their ten kids who resented my taking food off the table. I joined the army the day I turned eighteen. My fiancée, Phoebe, was my high school sweetheart. She waited for me to come home from overseas. She was relocated to a portal city when I was twenty-two, and I moved with her. She died because I failed to protect her."

Engaged. To someone else. Jealousy warred with pity, so bright and bitter that it snatched her breath away. It wasn't fair, it wasn't kind, but there it was. "What happened to her?"

"The ogre invasion of Bitter Hills."

Zoey winced. That had been a bad one. There had been a magical flare-up in the Chaos Realm, tearing open the portal near Bitter Hills, Colorado, until it was triple the size it had been. Ogres had flooded through in the hundreds. Thousands of humans had died.

Dominic grimaced and looked away. "Unfortunately, I survived it. Barely. The ogre picked me up and threw me fifty feet. I heard her die, Zoey. I heard her scream, and then I didn't hear anything." He shuddered, and the color drained from his face. "I was in the hospital for weeks. When I got out, I decided to go wolf. I didn't expect to survive the transition; I didn't care either way. But I knew I never wanted to feel that helpless again. You can't win against magic in a fair fight, so I needed to be magic myself. I wanted to be able to protect those I care about."

"I'm very sorry. I'm not going to lie to you … part of me is really jealous. I know that's not fair at all. It's horrible, really. I just … it feels so good to have you love me, Dominic. It really does." Her eyes filled with tears. "I want all of you."

He cupped her chin in his hand, and all the love in the world poured out of him. She could feel it warming her and filling her.

"You have all of me. You are my everything." He paused and looked at the door.

"What is it?" She followed his glance.

"I just wanted to make sure that son of a bitch Romano didn't sneak back up here and eavesdrop. It's okay, he didn't. If he was there, he couldn't stop himself from chiming in about how he told me so. And I'd be skinning myself a new rug."

Zoey burst out laughing. Tears streamed down her cheeks, dammed-up emotion flowing from her. There were many scary things in Encantado, but the only thing that had genuinely terrified her lately was the fear Dominic would never open himself up to her.

"I'll get you tissues." Dominic hurried to the kitchen and returned with a box.

"I love you so much." She sniffled and dabbed at her face. "Tell me about the wolf bite. About bonding."

He frowned. "When we shift to our wolf form and bite a female hard enough to break the skin, no matter the time of month, it forms a mate bond. That's why we're very careful not to bite a female accidentally. I know you've seen playful nips, but we have enough control over our animal to make sure it doesn't go too far. Once we've mate-bitten, the wolf craves the female's presence. It becomes attuned to her feelings and wants to please her. And if the female is a wolf, which most of the time it is, she instinctively reciprocates. If she's human, her feelings have to develop more naturally, and it takes longer. I should have been more sensitive to that."

"We'll work it out. Maybe … maybe it would be better if we left and went to some other portal city until this feud is over." She shook her head. "No, I can't because my friends are stuck here. Will Arturo let them stay with him?"

"Yes. Once he offers his protection, he wouldn't withdraw it without reason. I'm the one he's angry at, not them."

"All right. Should we tell Romano to come back in?"

Dominic grinned fiercely. "Hell no."

"Ooh. I know that look. It's a little scary." She returned his grin. "I like it."

Tenderly, he pulled down her pants, and she stepped out of them. Then he grabbed her shirt and ripped it open, buttons flying off.

"Dominic!" she screeched.

"Sorry." He smiled. "I'm an animal. Can't help myself when I'm around you."

"I forgive you ... on one condition. There's something I've been wanting to do since the first time I laid eyes on you."

Before he could speak, she sank down on her knees in front of him and unbuttoned his pants.

"Oh God," he groaned. "Zoey, I should be the one pleasing you, since you're my ... oh, baby."

His protests ended when she took him in her mouth, swirling her tongue over the thick head of his cock. She lapped up the pearl of pre-cum, and then traced the rim of his cock with the tip of her tongue.

His labored breathing sent flashes of pleasure through her body. She took him into her mouth again and tipped back her head, letting him thrust into her as he held her head in place.

"So. Fucking. Good."

Zoey moved her head in rhythm, her cheeks hollowing as she sucked. His breath quickened, and she stroked his balls with her fingers, lightly scraping her nails against the sensitive flesh.

"Zoey!" Dominic cried out, and she felt his balls tighten.

He tried to pull out of her mouth, but she grabbed his hips and held him in place, and he came—hard. She swallowed every drop of his release, and he stood there shuddering and panting, stroking her head.

"Fucking hell," he groaned finally, and then grabbed her and threw her over his shoulder in a fireman's carry.

"Hey!" she squealed as he carried her into the bedroom.

Dominic grunted out two words that let her know she was in for a world of pleasure and maybe a little bit of delicious pain.

"My turn."

CHAPTER *TWENTY-TWO*

"Oh God, so good," Zoey moaned. "More. Don't stop. Don't stop, Dominic!"

Dominic looked down at her empty plate. "You really like my cooking, don't you?"

She jammed her fork into the pancakes and flashed him a grin. "Just keep feeding me the deliciousness, and nobody gets hurt."

She was glad they had the apartment to themselves. Romano, under great protest, had been sent packing last night so Dominic could molest Zoey without Romano hearing and yelling his approval. He had gone back to pack property but insisted he'd return in the afternoon so he and Dominic could talk about their future.

Dominic slid his spatula under the pancakes on the frying pan and expertly flipped three more onto her plate.

As he joined her at the table, Zoey poured on syrup and slathered on butter. She took a bite of fluffy pancake and groaned in appreciation.

"That's right. Eat up. You'll need your strength. I've got plans for you." He waggled his eyebrows lasciviously.

"I'm about to get married to an insatiable pervert," she said. "How did I get so lucky?" She licked butter off her lip, then realized his gaze was suddenly focused on her mouth.

"You're going to lick me like that after breakfast," he assured her. "And I've got some creative ideas for the maple syrup."

"It'll get the sheets all sticky!" she protested.

"True," he conceded. "Okay, we can do that part in the bathtub. Don't try to argue with me," he added sternly. "Arguing with your mate is a punishable offense."

She ran her tongue around her lips and was rewarded by hearing him suck in his breath.

"But how will you punish me?" she teased.

His lips curled up in a smile, which quickly faded. His gaze flicked toward the window to the left.

"What?" She followed his gaze but didn't see anything.

"Did you hear that siren?"

"Not this time, but now that you mention it, I have heard more sirens than usual this morning, headed north." Their gazes met across the table. North. Toward the area where she'd lived up until very recently, where a lot of her friends still lived.

They had both turned off their phones last night. They hadn't watched television either. The entire city could be burning down.

"I've heard a lot more sirens than you have," Dominic said. "I wasn't really paying attention at first. But …" His brow wrinkled. "I am going to call Romano." He hurried over to his cell phone where it was charging on the counter and pressed the power button. "I will have him watch over you while I go north. I don't want to leave you, but I have an obligation to the city."

As he spoke, sirens blared.

Zoey hadn't heard those sounds in months, and never this far south. *Shelter in place. Magical emergency.*

Whoop, whoop, whoop.

Three siren blasts, then a pause. She was used to only one siren blast at a time. Three blasts meant a city-wide alarm. She'd never experienced one of those. That was bad. Some of her friends were still at Arturo's, which was built like a fortress and could probably withstand dragon-fire, but a lot of them were still in District 17.

What could it be? Trolls, ghouls, dragons, ogres? It could be anything.

Someone started pounding on the door. Dominic sniffed the air as he hurried to answer.

"Arturo," he said and yanked open the door.

Arturo loomed in the doorway, eyes blazing with an eerie glow. Carlo and Ottavio and a half-dozen foot soldiers stood in the hallway behind him.

"There are dozens of ghouls and at least five ogres rampaging the city," he said quickly. "Giuliana escaped my guards and headed up there so she could start healing. My men can't find her. I've been trying to call you. We're heading up there now."

"You left me on my own after my mate was kidnapped," Dominic said. "And it's your overbearing nature that drove Giuliana to run out there on her own, without the protection of the pack. If anything happens to her, it's on you."

"Let me at him! I'll fucking kill him!" Ottavio howled.

Arturo sent a blast of power at him, and Ottavio's howl ended in a yelp.

"I will help find her," Zoey offered.

"You're right, and I was wrong." Arturo spoke so fast his words were blurring together. "When it comes to Giuliana, I lose common sense. It was not your fault she left my house; it was mine, and I punished you for my mistake. I apologize." He inclined his head to the side, exposing his neck to Dominic. Zoey knew that show of submission was an enormous deal for the *Capo di tutti Capi*. "If you help her, I'll reinstate you into the pack."

"I gave you my loyalty and pledged my life to you for the last decade, and you abandoned me when I needed you most. I will never be part of your pack again, Arturo." Dominic's voice was thick with fury. "I will work with you to find her because she is my friend. And I will help take down the ghouls because it is the right thing to do. And then we're done."

"I'm coming! You need me. I can find her," Zoey said.

Dominic looked as if he wanted to argue, but Arturo said, "My men will make sure she's safe."

They followed Arturo out the door, crowded into a giant SUV, and drove north. Another car full of his men trailed behind them.

Cop cars and ambulances zipped through the mostly abandoned streets. Cars were parked haphazardly, many in no-parking zones. Storefronts were covered with steel shutters, and their protection wards glowed fiercely. Customers were most likely crowded inside, waiting fearfully and trying to reach their loved ones by phone. Signs blinked over designated shelter areas. As they drove, they saw a few doors open with people standing in them, waving in any stragglers. Homeowners took in any strangers who'd been caught far from their own homes when the sirens went off. Times like this were terrifying, but they also brought out the best in people. Differences vanished, and the city united to fight off the threat.

They took the road northeast through Bianchi Pack territory, but during a city-wide alert, all hostilities would be suspended.

They passed through the modest suburbs with their smaller houses. Bicycles lay abandoned on sidewalks. A woman rushed out into her front yard, grabbed a yapping collie, and ran back into her house before slamming her door.

Arturo's driver pulled into the parking lot of a warehouse next to a wooded area. A command center had been established there, and police, shifters, and mages rushed to-and-fro.

There was a row of bodies under tarps to one side of an asphalt lot. Med-mages and EMTs treated bleeding victims who had been grouped together in a triage area.

They all scrambled out of the SUV, Dominic keeping Zoey by his side. Arturo's foot soldiers crowded around him, awaiting orders.

"I don't like you being here. I should have just had you call me with her location," Dominic said to Zoey, tension vibrating through his body.

"That wouldn't work as well and you know it," she replied. "I've been focusing on her the whole ride up here. She's been moving around, and I'd have to keep calling you back to tell you her latest location. She's not the only person who might need to be found."

"We need to go get her, now," Arturo growled. His eyes glowed so brightly, they could have illuminated a ballroom.

Shouts and screams from the wooded area to their right distracted them. Arturo jerked, his nostrils flaring.

"She's not there. She's to the left," Zoey said.

"Go help," Arturo said, pointing his foot soldiers in the direction of the screaming. They tried to argue, clearly unhappy about leaving their leader unprotected, but he bellowed, "Don't fucking question me!" and sent a wave of skull-rattling power rolling over them.

They shifted without another word and ran in the direction he'd pointed. Zoey quickly led Arturo, Ottavio, Carlo, and Dominic into the wooded area to the left. She wrinkled her nose. The air reeked of ghoul.

They kept pushing through underbrush until they found Giuliana in a clearing, crouched over an injured, glassy-eyed human on a stretcher. There were EMTs and cops there too.

Giuliana ignored them as they rushed over to her. She poured all of her energy into healing the man, and as Zoey watched, blood stopped flowing from his gashes and his color went from waxy to merely pale.

"He's stable now," Giuliana pronounced.

The EMTs lifted the stretcher and hurried through the woods.

A terrible odor washed over them, and three ghouls came crashing through the bushes and headed straight for them. They were tall and cadaverously thin, their mouths filled with too many sharp, pointy teeth. Their eyes were pits of pure blackness, their hair yellowing, greasy strands plastered to their heads. They were naked, but their genitals were so shriveled, it was impossible to tell their sex.

Zoey tensed as all the wolves shifted and attacked the ghouls, tearing into them. The smell in the air was so ripe and horrible, it made her gag. It made her yearn for the scent of three-month-old garbage ripening in the sun on her neighborhood streets.

And then it was over. Ghouls were mindless rage machines, and all they did was lunge at things and tear at them with their claws and fangs. They couldn't plan or strategize in a fight, they didn't dodge or feint or flee, so they were easy for wolves to take down. Once their heads had been ripped off, they stopped moving but continued stinking.

"Gah," Zoey said, breathing through her mouth as she made her way back to Dominic. "That stench."

Arturo started to say something, and Dominic barked, "Quiet!"

Ottavio and Carlo snarled at Dominic for snapping at their Alpha.

"What is it?" Arturo demanded.

Dominic concentrated. "There's a portal close by. I can feel it. Believe me, when you've been partway through a portal, you don't forget how that feels."

Arturo nodded. "I sense it too. Powerful pulses of magic. Definitely a lesser portal, but I can sense chaos magic leaking through.

There's something strange about it though. Lesser portals usually fade at a steady rate. They don't pulse."

"We need to investigate." Ottavio turned and hurried through the woods, and Carlo followed him.

Zoey narrowed her eyes. *That's odd. He's leaving Arturo's side in the middle of a magical meltdown?*

Giuliana jumped up and followed Ottavio and Carlo, and Dominic hesitated and then grabbed Zoey's arm. They pushed through thick underbrush, made their way around a hillside, and … there it was. The portal was a bizarre rip in reality, a big hole about eight feet high and equally wide. It hurt to look directly at it, and the air in the clearing was wavery.

Standing near it, pointing a long, slim wand at the portal, was Benedict. His hand shook. His face was pale and sweat beaded on his forehead.

"Close it!" Arturo shouted.

"Can't you see I'm trying! I'm not strong enough on my own!" Benedict's hair was plastered to his skull with sweat.

A strangled scream came from the woods off to their left. "Primo," Arturo said. "That's his scent."

Zoey turned her gaze on Ottavio. *He's behaving oddly.*

He had stepped close to Arturo, but he was putting Arturo between him and the portal. He *should* be placing his body between Arturo and the source of danger. Arturo, distracted, took a couple of steps backward—closer to the portal.

Dominic noticed at the same time. "Stop that!" he bellowed at Ottavio.

"Stop what?" Ottavio replied innocently.

"We need to get help for Benedict," Arturo growled. "A few more mages will be able to help him close it."

"No, we need to stay here in case more ghouls come out," Ottavio reasoned.

Arturo looked at him strangely. "Since when do you argue with me?"

A strange question bubbled up inside Zoey's head. It had been nagging at her subconscious for a while now, but all of a sudden it seemed extremely urgent. "Giuliana, how many times did you follow me and try to kidnap me?" she blurted.

"She did what?!" Dominic barked.

"You're asking me this now?" Giuliana squinted at the portal, then looked at Zoey, blinking hard. "Twice. Why?"

"There were dozens of times something was blocking me, trying to get at me. For weeks. Ever since Dominic bit me. It was you, wasn't it, Ottavio?" Zoey demanded. "You're up to something."

They were distracted for a minute when Luigi Bianchi came bursting through the bushes, grinning fiercely, covered with blood. "It's done," he said to Ottavio. "I killed them."

Primo and anyone who tried to defend him. Zoey's stomach clenching tightly.

Quick as a flash, Ottavio jammed his pistol against Giuliana's head. Giuliana cried out with rage, clawing at Ottavio's hands. Arturo let out an infuriated snarl.

"Careful," Ottavio snapped. "A silver bullet through the skull and she's beyond the help of any med-mage."

Dominic moved protectively in front of Zoey, putting himself between her and Ottavio.

"Why?" Arturo demanded, his eyes glowing a deadly gold.

"Because you are weak," Ottavio said. "And so was Primo. You should have killed Primo and taken the east side for the pack a long time ago. Primo should have been willing to do the same or die trying. No real Alpha allows another pack to operate in their territory."

Carlo looked hurt and baffled. "What are you doing?" he demanded of his brother. "Why are you hurting Giuli?"

Ottavio ignored him and looked at Arturo with hatred. "You should have killed Carlo when he failed the turn. He's an embarrassment. A weakness."

"Me?" Carlo's face fell. "I'm barrassment? Is that bad?"

"Stop him!" Dominic bellowed to Benedict.

Benedict glanced at Ottavio. "Hurry the fuck up," he snapped. "I can't hold the portal open much longer."

"Holy hell," Zoey said in astonishment.

Benedict was working with Ottavio and Luigi. He wasn't trying to close the portal; he was using his magic to keep it open. He'd been tearing open portals and releasing ghouls. Distracting the authorities while the two packs duked it out, and while Ottavio and Luigi maneuvered behind the scenes.

MATED to the ENFORCER

Ottavio started moving with Giuliana, forcing her toward the portal. "Why were you following me?" Zoe tried to stall him.

"Because you are a troublemaker who asks questions."

"*You*," Arturo said furiously. "You were the one who drove the businesses out of town. You sabotaged the garbage pickup. You told Jordan to stop the garbage trucks, and then you killed him so he couldn't snitch on you. You were trying to turn me against Dominic and weaken the pack."

"Only so I could build it back up again!" Ottavio yelled, his face reddening. "Luigi and I are going to unite the packs and eliminate the weaklings. The whole city will bow to us. Anyone who doesn't like it will die. Just like this spoiled little bitch."

He hurled Giuliana through the portal and into the Chaos Realm.

Without a word, Arturo dove in after her.

"I can get them! I can get them!" Zoey screamed at Dominic. "My map magic will bring us back! Stay out, Dominic!" Before he could stop her, she darted through.

But Dominic, that fool, ran in after her.

Bizarre sensations blasted Zoey, overwhelming her. The ground rippled under her feet. Her head pounded, and she choked on a wave of nausea and terror. If Benedict stopped focusing his magic, the portal would seal itself off. And that's what he would do, of course. They'd be trapped here forever, and Ottavio could spin his own story about what had happened and take over the pack. The portal wouldn't close instantly, but without Benedict holding it open, they probably only had minutes.

Everything was wavy and fractured and constantly changing. She fell to her knees, disoriented, and started crawling toward where she thought Giuliana was, but her map magic was confused. It wanted her to run in a thousand directions at once.

What was she crawling on? The ground felt harsh and spiky, ugly and angry. The air here hated her. This place was wrong, or she was wrong. She needed to get out, get out, get out …

Zoey desperately tried to focus. She pictured Giuliana, but the picture stayed still in her mind. She couldn't sense which way to go. That had never happened to her before. She was completely lost.

She forced herself to crawl. Anything was better than staying still. She'd find her friends or die trying. She blindly thrust out her hands, crawling on her knees, desperate to feel anything. The air slid through her fingers with a strange, oily sensation.

She couldn't see. There were no colors or shapes anymore, and everything was blurring together. She heard distorted howling sounds, and she thought it was Dominic yelling her name, but she was no longer sure of anything.

Zoey had led the man she loved to his death. She had failed everyone. Her heart sped up, slowed down, fell out of her body, jumped and danced … she was losing her mind. They would all die here.

CHAPTER TWENTY-THREE

"Come on!" That sounded like Carlo's voice. Sort of like Carlo, but clear and intelligent, all the dullness gone. It must be a trick of the Chaos Realm. "I've got you! Zoey, come on! This way!"

The air was too thick to breathe. Zoey couldn't move her limbs. It felt as if someone was pulling her through mud, through quicksand, through … through the portal.

She and Dominic flew through the air and landed with heavy thuds on the dirt, gasping for breath. A minute later, Arturo and Giuliana flew out. Dominic reached out and grabbed Zoey's trembling arm and pulled her to him.

"Oh my God. What was that?" she moaned, half-dazed.

"You're alive. You're alive," Dominic chanted, pressing his face into her hair.

The air smelled like blood. Carlo was saying something, and then he was standing over her.

A small explosion shook the ground. Zoey looked up, and the portal was gone. Benedict lay on the ground, his throat torn open. Luigi was sprawled on the grass next to him, his neck hanging at a strange angle, and Ottavio was on his knees, whimpering and clutching a broken arm.

"I said, are you all right?" Carlo said again.

"All right?" Zoey blinked up at him. "I … I can breathe. I can see again." She felt her face, her legs. "I'm here. All of me is here. Whoa. That was so much fun, let's never do it again." She struggled to stand.

Dominic climbed to his feet, and they stood there, leaning on each other and shaking.

"Carlo?" Arturo stood, looking dazed. "Carlo! You're healed. My God, you're back."

Carlo nodded slowly. "When I jumped through the portal after you, everything was perfectly clear. You were all crawling around yelling in this strange, blank land where everything had no color. It was like the chaos was scrambling your brains and fixing mine."

He looked around the clearing. "I killed them," he said dimly, his gaze focusing on Benedict and Luigi.

Giuliana was still on her hands and knees, puking in the grass.

"Carlo," Ottavio wailed, cradling his shattered arm. "Look what you've done! *To me*! I'm your brother!"

"No, Ottavio. Look what *you've* done." Carlo's face was bleak as he stalked over to Ottavio. He pointed in the direction of the city. "You had Benedict open the gates to hell. All those people died just so you could lure Arturo here. You knew he'd have to respond to a ghoul attack, and then you'd throw him through the portal. That was the only way you could kill him, wasn't it? You couldn't take him on in a fair fight."

"Carlo, you're fixed! You're okay now!" Ottavio tried to scoot away from his brother. He gave him a sickly, ingratiating grin, cringing as Carlo followed him. "Look how strong you are! You're stronger than ever! We can rule the pack together now! We can … *ahhhhhhh …*"

Zoey put her hands over her ears to dull the sound of Ottavio's dying screams as his brother killed him.

Two days later, they were gathered in Arturo's living room. Arturo had summoned Dominic, Romano, and Zoey to his house, probably to ask Dominic to rejoin the pack. That wasn't an offer Dominic could accept. He'd only come to say goodbye.

Giuliana was there, sitting to the left of her uncle, still looking pale and queasy, as they all were. Even Arturo's normally healthy complexion had a pallor to it. Med-mages had done everything they could, but they'd all feel like they had a bad hangover for at least another few days.

Carlo sat by Arturo's right side. His demeanor had changed so much, he was barely recognizable. He wore a crisp, pressed suit, and his dark eyes shone with intelligence and awareness, but they were haunted. Ottavio's treachery had cut deep, and having to kill his own brother would always weigh heavily on Carlo's soul.

They sat nibbling on biscotti and sipping coffee for a few minutes, murmuring pleasantries, while Dominic waited for Arturo to get to the point of why he'd invited them.

But the question he sprang on him wasn't the one Dominic expected.

"Why did you bite Zoey?" Arturo asked. "It wasn't a moon-bite."

Dominic set down his coffee and arched an eyebrow. "How long have you known?"

Zoey looked at him in confusion.

"I always knew," Arturo said, leaning back in his seat. "You're not a born wolf. You're a made wolf. Only born wolves moon-bite."

"Why didn't you say anything?" Dominic tilted his head and quirked a brow.

Arturo shrugged. "It gave us an easy way to get out of having you enter an alliance with Fabiana. I knew they only wanted to do it to send her in as a spy. I suspected they might use it as an excuse to declare war on us, but they would have done so either way. I also suspected they were somehow behind the sabotage on our businesses, I just never guessed Ottavio was part of that too."

"I knew too," Giuliana said. "It's just not something that comes up that often because made wolves are rarer than born wolves, and either way, most wolves end up in arranged matings before they get to meet their real mate on a full moon. But I knew it was impossible it was a moon-bite. That's why I questioned it. I thought Zoey had placed a spell on you or something and she was just playing coy to make it more believable."

"So this was never real?" Zoey's eyes shimmered with tears. Dominic shot Arturo a dirty look. He wished Arturo had let him tell Zoey on his own, without springing it on her like this.

"My feelings for you have always been real," Dominic said fiercely. "And once I shifted and bit you, my wolf took to you right away."

Zoey blinked harder, and it hurt Dominic's heart to see her questioning their mating bond. "But why did you even bite me in the first place?"

"Because Ottavio was going to kill you. I saw you walk up to him and ask for an audience with Arturo. He was just about to shift and kill. I know exactly what he looks like when he's about to do that. I've seen him do it many times before."

She sucked in a breath. "You're kidding me. He would have killed me on the spot?"

"He was seconds away from tearing out your throat. I thought he believed you were being disrespectful to Arturo. Now, I realize he didn't want Arturo to start looking into the garbage situation. But when I saw that look on his face, I acted on instinct. To protect you. The only way to prevent him from killing you was to shift and mate-bite you."

"But … that's for life!" she spluttered. She looked at him with a hint of doubt. "Isn't it?"

He grabbed her hand and squeezed it. "There's nowhere in the world you could run and hide from me, Zoey. You are mine. I meant it when I said I was entranced by you the first moment I ever saw you. I wanted you so much, it was painful for me to talk to you, so I avoided you. I thought about you all the time, but I was willing to sacrifice my happiness for the good of the pack. Then, when I saw Ottavio about to rip off your head, I just … acted. My wolf and I, together. I have never regretted it."

"I have another favor to ask of you," Arturo said, and Dominic tensed. It wouldn't be easy to turn down Arturo after living his life only for the Moretti Pack for the last ten years.

But Arturo shocked him, yet again. "Primo's death has created a power vacuum in the East. The Bianchi Pack has been dismantled, and the surviving Bianchi family members have fled, scattering around the country. The remaining pack members need a leader. You will take over as *Capo di tutti Capi* of the Lombardi Pack, with Romano as your *Capo*, and I would like you to take Giuliana as your healer."

"My brains must still be scrambled from the Chaos Realm," Dominic said. "I could swear I just heard you say you wanted me to take over the former Bianchi Pack."

"You heard me perfectly well." Arturo's amber eyes shone fiercely.

He meant it. Dominic would be *Capo di tutti Capi* of his own pack. He'd never even aspired to that. He'd been content leading his own small crew of soldiers and being fiercely loyal to his boss.

"I don't know if I'm cut out for it," he protested. "I'm nothing like you."

"You don't have to be. No two leaders are exactly like, but the important thing is, you've got the right qualities to lead a pack. You're strong, fearless, and capable. You're harsh but fair. You're well-known and well-respected in the city. There is no-one else I'd rather see as leader. You and I would be able to work in cooperation, rather than competing with each other. No more pack wars. No more wasting time and money when we could be working together and boosting our bottom line. No more crying widows." Arturo scowled. "They're so loud when they cry. I find it distracting."

Yep, that was Arturo—all heart.

Dominic looked at Zoey. "My mate would have to agree to this. Asking her to be the Alpha's mate is a lot."

"It's …" Zoey looked slightly panicked and gulped a deep breath. "It would mean peace for the city, wouldn't it? Peace for the packs? If so, I'm willing to try my best."

"You think they would even accept me as their Alpha?" Doubt wracked Dominic's voice.

"With me backing it, yes. This would allow them to stay in their homes and keep their property. If you're not the leader, there's a power vacuum, and who knows what they'd end up with?" Arturo looked at his niece. "And you, my darling. I know it's time to let you free to live your own life. As long as you're under my roof, I can't resist my urge to protect you so much that I'm smothering you. It is agonizingly hard to let you go, but it is what is best for you."

"Uncle," she said and hugged him, crying. "I know you did it because you love me. You did the wrong thing for the right reasons. Thank you."

"I'm a *Capo*?" Romano said, looking comically happy.

"This is what you focus on?" Dominic said, irritated. "*If* I decide to take over the east side, and that's a big if, then you're only a *Capo* until you push my wolf too far and I fit you with concrete galoshes and feed you to a kraken."

"Excellent!" Romano tried to fist-bump him. Dominic ignored it. "I should last a good year, at least. Maybe two."

"Optimistic," Dominic muttered. "I still didn't say I'd do it. I need a few days to think about it, Arturo, but I appreciate your faith in me."

He stood, and Zoey joined him, grimacing. "Frickin' hell," she groaned. "Chaos Realm hangover suuucks."

"I hear that," Dominic said. "I feel like a thousand-year-old wolf with arthritis. Right now, I couldn't be the Alpha of a Cub Scout pack."

"Sorry I missed it," Romano said cheerfully, rising to his feet. "The Chaos Realm is so much fun. Do you want me to carry you? Can I get a walker for you, grandpa?"

"You can get a head start before I kick your tail," Dominic growled.

As they limped toward the door, Zoey's phone rang with the "Mama Mia" ringtone. Her mother had called multiple times since the ghoul attack made the news, each time wanting reassurance her oldest daughter was still breathing and mostly intact. Dominic grabbed the phone from Zoey.

"Dominic! If you embarrass me, I will cut you!" Zoey hissed.

"Mrs. Monroe," he said, smirking at Zoey. "So glad you called! Are you having a nice day? I have news for you. You're going to need to make space in your calendar for a wedding."

Epilogue

Zoey and Kalinda took a seat at a corner table at the trendy new coffee shop, The Daily Grind. There was a line down the block and a two-hour waiting list for lunch, but Zoey knew the owners. She was also the mate of the Lombardi Pack *Capo*, so one table was roped off and sat empty when she wasn't there, always available for her.

The ghoul attack of the spring had made international news. The neighborhood's proximity to the portal had given it a weird kind of cachet.

The odds of another attack were unlikely, but there was still that rollercoaster thrill of being near something so potentially perilous. Trendy boutiques were springing up, and homeowners gave paid tours of the ghoul-invaded neighborhoods, where all the damage had been carefully preserved.

Giuliana had opened up a consignment store, selling off all of her designer clothes. She no longer had Arturo's limitless credit card at her disposal, but she turned out to have a great eye for vintage and gently used items. When she wasn't working as a healer, she was scouring thrift shops for new items to snap up, upcycle, and sell.

Kalinda had entered into a lucrative partnership with The Daily Grind, and they carried a line of her home-baked goods and provided the gourmet coffee for her catering events. They were looking to go national.

Kalinda had also, of course, catered the enormous wedding bash thrown by Dominic and the Lombardi Pack. Zoey's entire family had attended, glowing with happiness, and now Dominic had permanently rented out an entire luxury suite for them in a southside hotel, so they could visit whenever they wanted.

"You guys!" Danielle called out, hurrying over to them with a tray. She set down two coffee cups and a carafe and handed them menus. "You look great, Zoey. Hey, Kalinda, love the new 'do."

Kalinda's hair was braided and piled up on top of her head in an elaborate bun.

"I do look pretty hot," Kalinda agreed. "The usual for me, Danielle. Sit down and hang out for a minute!"

Danielle sank into a chair and stole Zoey's coffee.

"Decaf!" Zoey called out to a waiter who hurried to get her a cup.

"The service in here is fantastic, if I do say so myself." Danielle drank half of Zoey's coffee in one gulp. "And this is orgasm in a cup."

"I'm worried about you," Zoey said to Danielle. "You haven't complained in weeks. Are you dying?"

The waiter set the decaf in front of Zoey, and she poured in creamer and took a sip.

"Well, opening my own coffee shop didn't exactly suck too much. And having it be the hottest hotspot in the city hasn't been too awful either."

Danielle had quit working at the weather department three months earlier when she and Tony opened The Daily Grind. She was indeed much happier these days. She looked fondly at Tony, who was a blur of motion working behind the counter. Dominic, as a favor to Zoey, had insisted Arturo let his chef come over to the Lombardi Pack. Arturo had done it, grudgingly, as an apology for kicking Dominic out of the Moretti Pack.

Tony was a broad-shouldered, handsome man in his forties, with long black hair pulled back in a ponytail. His goatee, streaked with one white stripe, gave him a devilish look. He winked at Danielle and blew her a kiss. "And Tony isn't the worst boyfriend in the world. You see those cream-filled cannolis?" She pointed at the glass dessert display and made a circle with her thumb and index figure. "Well, let me tell you …"

"Argh! TMI!" Zoey cried out at the exact same moment Kalinda leaned forward, eyes gleaming, and said, "Go on."

Fortunately, they were briefly distracted when Cin and Lorenzo strolled hand in hand through the door, chatting happily. Lorenzo had completed his first semester with excellent grades at Encantado Technical Institute. Dominic's whispered threats probably had something to do with that. Lorenzo had set up a website for Cin to sell her jewelry, and Dominic had bought a house for their former street kid friends to live in. A couple of them had accepted his offer to put them through school, and the others were working for the pack.

Zoey had wheedled and cajoled and finally managed to convince both of the packs to make apartments available to all of the castaway kids in pack territory. The kids were required to do cleanup in their neighborhoods to contribute toward their rent and food. Not all of the kids accepted the offer, but a fair amount of them did. Arturo had done it grudgingly because he didn't like giving away anything for free. In the end, it generated public good will for the packs because it lowered the rate of burglaries and vandalism.

A lot of the kids worked at the Lombardi Community Garden, helping to grow organic vegetables. That was where Zoey could usually be found during the day, ensuring the greenery stayed green.

Andrea and Stewart were away on their honeymoon, so Cin and Lorenzo were staying at Zoey and Dominic's until they got back. Lorenzo wanted to propose to Cin, but Dominic had strongly suggested he wait until he graduated. Dominic's word was law as far as Lorenzo was concerned.

Lorenzo and Cin stopped by their table to say hi, and then went to the bakery counter to place a to-go order.

"By the way, since when do you drink decaf?" Danielle arched an eyebrow.

"You guys make amazing decaf. Too much caffeine later in the day keeps people up at night." Zoey avoided Danielle's gaze. "Oh look, there's my mate! God, he's sexy. Isn't he sexy?" She smiled at Dominic, who was heading their way with Romano.

"Not half as sexy as my Tony, but I mean, I don't puke when I look at him or anything," Danielle said. "And I know when you're dodging a question."

The crowd parted like the Red Sea for Dominic and Romano, looking at them with mingled fear and admiration. Zoey still felt a little badly that people were terrified of her mate, but she also knew if they weren't, he wouldn't be able to maintain control of the pack.

The two men grabbed chairs and pulled them up to the table, and Dominic kissed Zoey on the lips.

"Hey, the hot chick used to be your boss, right?" Romano said to Zoey.

Kalinda tried to look annoyed rather than pleased, and mostly succeeded. She snapped her fingers in front of Romano's face.

"The hot chick is sitting right here," she said. "She can hear you."

"Did you ever tell her about the time I almost ate her?" Romano grinned at Danielle, and Dominic punched him in the arm. "What did I say?" Romano's brow wrinkled in puzzlement.

"*What did you say?*" Kalinda demanded, straightening up and shoving her chair back several inches.

Romano gave Kalinda a long, lingering look as she picked up her coffee and took a sip. "Hmm. Still not too late for that to happen."

Kalinda choked on her coffee and slammed the mug down on the table. "Prepare yourself. I am going to smack the living shiznit out of your friend," she informed Zoey.

"It'll just hurt your hand. Believe me, I know," Zoey said. "Although I completely understand the urge."

Kalinda tried anyway, slapping Romano in the face. Romano smiled politely.

"That tickled, a little," he said.

"Dammit," she scowled, shaking her hand.

Danielle made a timeout motion with her hands, forming the letter T. "Hey! Excuse me! Dominic and Zoey! Do you guys have something you want to tell me?" she demanded.

The chatter at the other tables died down a little, and people pretended not to listen.

"Do we?" Dominic looked at his mate, puzzled.

"Well, it's a little early," Zoey muttered, cheeks reddening. "But since Nancy Drew figured it out, the reason I'm switching to decaf is …"

"No!" Danielle gasped dramatically.

"Shut the front door!" Kalinda echoed Danielle's gasp, pretending to clutch at her chest. Everyone at the tables around them stopped pretending not to listen and stared at them breathlessly, waiting.

"Yes." Zoey nodded and tenderly patted her stomach. "I'm late. And I'm never late."

"You mean we …" Dominic's face lit up.

"Yes. We're going to have a little baby *Capo*."

THE END

DO YOU WANT MORE OF THE PORTAL CITY PROTECTORS?

Click here
for Romano's story.
Keep reading for
Chapter One of
Mated to the Enforcer.

CHAPTER ONE

"Not now," Kalinda Thorton muttered under her breath. "Anytime but now."

Her magic was a fickle bitch. Weak and barely noticeable most of her life, it had been flaring up explosively for the last few months at the worst possible moments. She felt the weird, prickly energy that warned her the strength of her magic was shooting through the roof for no logical reason, which meant her coordination would be wobbly and spills were a serious risk.

She smoothed down her black tuxedo jacket over her black skirt and slowly counted to ten. When that didn't work, she rubbed the tingling spot over her heart and took a deep breath. Kalinda had been dealing with aggravating heart palpitations, tingling, and weird bursts of her normally less-than-stellar magical ability.

Running Kalinda's Katering in Encantado, Nevada, was a headache to begin with. Portal cities weren't all glitz and glamour like the outside world believed. Battles, attacks, and paying for protection all ran rampant in the city of sin.

Kalinda stood straight and, by sheer effort of will, forced her hands to stop trembling. *Just a couple of hours and then on to the next client, K. You've got this.*

Kalinda stopped long enough to check her braid wasn't out of place in the mirror then went on her way to check on her guests.

Rock Landing was *the* place for Viscount Pride parties, and she'd served here often enough to have the layout memorized.

One platter, a delicious Thai noodle in spicy peanut sauce, was left to the side, and she grabbed it, stifling the urge to fuss. The Leo of the Viscount Pride shouldn't have been left waiting to be served.

"Table two is looking for another helping. Get it done," Silva called, her short legs already carrying her away and out of the preparation area as the other servers plated her requests. Kalinda grabbed it, happy at least one of her girls was moving and getting stuff done.

"I've got table two. Keep going with the rest," Kalinda ordered and headed out.

A loud buzz of conversation thrummed in her ears. The pride was rowdy. Some were eating, while others mingled and joked, and a pair of lionesses circled each other readying to start a mock fight over a plate of steak tartare between them.

What is it with cats and playing with their food?

Kalinda danced around them, setting table two's plate down with a flourish. "Enjoy!"

The young cub at the table growled his thanks, and she continued on her way.

Okaaaaaaaaaay.

The Leo, Orion Viscount, sat in a throne-like chair, wrapped in a custom-cut tan suit that did nothing but blend with the blond mane around his shoulders. The thick waves were shaggy and rough, just like the animal that lived within him, and his rounded ears stuck out. He surveyed the happenings around him from his elevated perch, a single round table in front of him and a female at his side. Kalinda thought they called their enforcers "chargers."

Built like an Amazon, and a head taller than Kalinda's own six feet, the charger turned her golden eyes on Kalinda and sniffed the air before nodding her head imperceptibly to continue. Prides tended to have a male at the head, with a few other males in positions of rank, but were mostly dominated by women.

Half the damn cubs here are probably the Leo's.

Orion Viscount drank his wine from an enormous glass and pretended he was too important to acknowledge Kalinda's approach. Whatever. His disdain didn't bother her. As her mother would have said: "*Consider the source.*"

Orion's eyes coldly swept the room as if he were thinking, "I pity you peons for not being able to sneeze on money and flush it down the toilet. Bwahahaha!"

"Your meal is served, Leo. I wanted to bring it personally and thank you for your continued use of Kalinda's Katering. If there is anything else, don't hesitate to ask."

Was that sarcasm? Nah, only in her head.

He finally turned his head and sniffed the air. "Your service is appalling, and your magic fouls the air, *mage*."

And you're about two seconds from having my stiletto in your eye, pussy cat.

Kalinda smiled sweetly. "Enjoy!"

She was not going to respond to him the way he deserved just because it would make her temporarily feel better. Any trouble she caused would rile up his pride and put her employees in danger, and her prime job was to protect her girls. Sure, they might have to deal with an occasional groping shifter or touchy daywalker, but she'd taught her girls how to handle them too.

A well-placed foot or elbow helped a lot of that.

Her cheeks were hurting from smiling so hard, and she turned to leave, but a sudden screech stopped her in her tracks. The room became deafeningly silent as she spun around.

"You've killed me."

The Leo's deep voice had suddenly gone high-pitched and whiny. She blinked for a few seconds, wondering exactly how the Leo had attained *that* level of octave before she snapped back reality.

"What? Are you okay?" Kalinda's heart raced.

He fanned himself and yanked at his tie, his face turning red as a tomato. Kalinda counted at least three large veins popping out on his forehead. His charger gripped his shoulders, keeping him upright as she growled at Kalinda.

What was going on?

"She's poisoned me!" Leo wheezed.

Kalinda shook her head. "I've done no such thing. What are you talking about?"

Orion jerked, his mouth opening and closing like a fish out of water before he slumped over dramatically. "Dead. I'm dead."

She would have laughed at the picture in front of her if she wasn't surrounded by pissed-off lions and lionesses with her staff's lives in the balance. Heat spread through her limbs, a sign her magic was about to pop a filter.

Great. Just great.

"Mr. Viscount, the meal was cooked and delivered just as you ordered. Your charger sniffed for anything out of the ordinary. If you need the assistance of Warlock Cyrus, he can be called immediately."

They were *shifters*. There was no way any ingredient in the food would have made it past their noses.

Kalinda turned and snapped her fingers at her girls, hoping they'd get the signal and go. Silva, her white hair pulled into a messy bun atop her head was the smallest of them all, her delicate pointy ears a sign of her Fae ancestry. But she was quick, darting between the shifters to each girl and yanking them behind her.

"I'll call Cyrus right away," Silva announced.

I'm giving that girl a raise.

The heat in Kalinda's body built, hotter and hotter, spiraling from her heart and out through her fingertips. Without thinking, she touched Orion, spreading magic to him as well.

Calm. Be calm and talk to me.

His eyes glazed over, and he smiled.

Orion started wheezing again and spluttered, "P-pretty. Such … dark … skin. Y-you're g-gorgeous. You want to be my Nubian princess?"

Whaaaat? No, he didn't. Seriously? Did he just go there?

Okay, that wasn't what she'd expected to happen.

"Thank you," she said with a tight-lipped smile. "Now, what's wrong with your food?"

"I could make you Prima."

As in the head female of a Pride? Um, no thank you.

She flashed him her most diplomatic smile. "I appreciate the offer. But first, let's talk about what's wrong, okay?"

"Remove your hands from the Leo!" The charger—what was her name? Oh, Roxi—jumped between Kalinda and Orion, breaking the connection. He immediately went back into spasms, flopping down to the ground and screaming again.

"You've poisoned me! I can't breathe. I'm dying. Can't you see

I'm dying?"

If you can talk, you can breathe. Melodramatic much?

Dang it, she wasn't supposed to be thinking like that. She took a deep breath and backed away from Roxi with her palms up in a placating gesture.

"I just wanted to make sure he was all right and see what the issue is. He ordered the Thai noodle in peanut sa—"

"*Peanuts.*"

Kalinda's ears were bleeding, she knew it, and she knew she heard several glasses shatter from Mr. Leo's newest interpretation of Minnie Riperton's skillset. Hitting high notes like that really should have crushed his vocal cords.

Hand to his chest, head screwed sideways, and his muzzle twisted up in the greatest affront, Outraged, Orion must have forgotten about not being able to breathe as he huffed at her, outraged.

"Just because you are friends with the Lombardi Pack Alpha bitch doesn't mean you are untouchable," Roxi hissed through a steadily morphing face.

"I didn't poison him!" she protested. "I gave him what he ordered."

"The Leo is allergic to peanuts. He never would have ordered it."

"I can show you the paperwork. Have someone follow me to my office. I'll prove it."

Was she terrified? Of course, but she didn't run a business in one of the most dangerous places in the world and maintain Level-7 wards on her windows in case of attack to back down at every challenge. Shifters were the worst with dominance and only understood things when they got knocked over the head.

She always knew she was on her own when it came to handling emergencies. In theory, the Mage Council provided protection, but they only came down for major squabbles between groups; they wouldn't waste their time on an issue like this. They'd rather let the pride get rid of her and be done with it.

Roxi nodded at someone behind Kalinda. "Take her, and kill her if the information is wrong."

Wonderful.

Kalinda turned on her heels, head held high, back straight, and floated. Her mother always told her a woman had to fight the whole world, and the best way to do it was with a smile, good character, and a hell of a walk.

She ignored the snapping shifters with each step and avoided the large beige lioness circle on the edge—they'd already shifted and were ready to attack. Kalinda put one foot in front of the other, hips swaying, and never looked anywhere but between the shoulder blades of the charger escorting her back into the serving room.

As they entered, Orion let out another piercing wail, and Kalinda grimaced.

"What room did you set up as your office?" the no-name-charger sneered at Kalinda. Her blond hair was cut close to the scalp, shoulders barely contained in her sleek mermaid style dress, and blood-red nails curled like claws.

"The Cub Area."

They had never let her into the inner sanctum of Rock Landing, instead keeping her to the children's space just off the kitchen and open ballroom. Kalinda was escorted into her makeshift office and went right to her papers. She found what she needed in one shuffle before handing it over.

"Here is the order list, signed and confirmed."

"We shall see."

Someone had their panties in a bunch.

What would Kalinda have to gain by killing Orion? If this was a plan to extort her, she'd find out who was behind it. There was no way in hell she was going to let her business reputation be destroyed by someone playing a game.

She was proud of how she'd managed to build up one of the most sought-after catering businesses from scratch after being forced to move to Encantado. And nobody would take that away from her.

Her magic, low as it was, had come to light while she was in culinary school. Luckily, she'd managed to graduate before the Federal Bureau of Magical Containment swept her out of her life and into a portal city.

Her dreams of owning a five-star restaurant in the Bay Area disappeared. Her fiancé had chosen not to come with her; he didn't want his children tainted by having "magic blood." She'd clawed her way to where she was now in Encantado, despite the loss of her mother a few years back, and she'd made it her mission to make Kalinda's a household name.

"It seems in order. Are there any other copies? A way you manipulated this receipt?"

"The signing isn't done until we get here, as always, and I have no access to a system here. Roxi signed off on the menu, as you can see. Please take up any discrepancies with her."

"Are you calling our head charger a traitor?"

Did. She. Just. Spit. On. Me?

"No, I'm saying Kalinda's Katering has done what was ordered and will be happy to serve another meal, if that's what you would prefer."

Suddenly, Kalinda began to sweat and breathe hard, as if she'd been transported into a sauna. Hot. It was so freaking hot. Her magic, which normally did nothing more than make her food more delicious and add a sense of comfort, pulsed under her skin. She resisted the urge to rake at her arms, but she couldn't stop the magic from leaking out. Finally, brilliant rays of gold and white spread from her, weaving its way around the charger in front of her and back out the door.

The charger dropped to the floor, purring, stretching her back, and kneading at the floor. Sharp nails curved from her fingertips and plucked at the rug. Kalinda took a step back, eyeing her suspiciously.

"Um, Kalinda? You may want to come out here," Silva called.

Kalinda stepped over the lioness currently humping the air in the middle of the floor and headed out into the prep area.

The room had gone crazy.

Silva, who had a knack for canceling magic not Fae based, was the only one standing. Literally. Kalinda's servers rolled on the floor, laughing and singing random songs, while the party outside had turned into Woodstock.

"What the hell?" Kalinda blinked hard and shook her head. Nope, not having an illusion. Gold and white ribbons danced over everyone, slipping over even Roxi and Orion, until the Leo had the aforementioned charger bent over the table and—

"All right, time to get out of here. Do you see the colors?"

Silva frowned at Kalinda. "What colors?"

"The gold and white lights. You don't see them?"

"Maybe a drug was filtered into the ventilation and you're affected too. I think we should all leave."

Kalinda shook her head, confused. She wasn't crazy—the magic flowing from her was in color and had caused everyone in the room to get frisky. Even the few cubs who'd been in attendance were outside, racing up and down a jungle gym Kalinda could see through a large bay window.

With shaking hands and a pounding heart, Kalinda did what she did best—direct.

Looking to her cooks and servers, she pointed to the front door. "Get out of here, now. There are vans waiting outside."

"But—"

"Don't argue. I'll meet you back at the shop." She would stay on scene and get what help she could. She couldn't just leave the Pride here in this state, especially knowing she'd probably caused it.

Kalinda was going to have to call her best friend Zoey and her mate Dominic. The Lombardi Pack was feared and respected throughout Encantado, and whatever was happening here, they'd be able to handle it.

She hoped. Of course, the price would be high—Zoey was going to give her grief for the rest of her life, and probably into the afterlife.

She knew it, but she picked up her spell phone and dialed anyway.

"Kalinda? Everything okay?"

"Well, that depends. I mean, it's only like I may have used magic to turn Rock Landing into a massive orgy after being accused of attempting to kill the Leo. I may have started an incident. Other than that, everything is peachy."

"You *what*?" Zoey squawked.

"Just come help me. Whenever this stuff calms down, they're probably going to want to kill me. I'd like to stay alive today."

"You're going to have to explain this better when we get there."

"Who are you bringing?" Kalinda felt a sudden flutter of alarm. "Not him. Don't say you're bringing him."

Zoey actually laughed, the wench. "Romano isn't going to pass up a chance to see this, not in a million years."

Ugh. Not Romano! The Lombardi Pack's enforcer was far too

arrogant, far too sexy for his own good—or hers, for that matter—and he was a total flirt. When he walked down the street, you could practically see women's panties melting. Well, that wouldn't happen with Kalinda. Not today, not ever. She'd already gone down the love 'em and get screwed over train. She wasn't interested in a second trip.

"You don't actually have to tell him about it," she argued.

"I have to tell my mate, and he tells Romano everything," Zoey protested with a laugh.

"Seriously?" Kalinda groaned. "I never should have warned you when the *Capo* came to claim you!"

"Ha! That's what friends are for, silly. That and having each other's backs. I've got yours."

A wave of dizziness rolled over Kalinda, and black spots swam in front of her eyes. She was going to fall and mess up her uniform. She *hated* being dirty. "Oh, that's good because I think I'm going to pass out."

Zoey's worried voice was very far away now. "Kalinda? Ka—"

Yep. Dry cleaning won't be getting these stains out.

End of sample.
Click here

to continue reading
Mated to the Enforcer,
Book 2 in the
Portal City Protectors series.

ABOUT THE AUTHOR

Georgette St. Clair writes hot, sexy romances starring Alpha heroes. The road to love may be rocky and fraught with peril (and humor and scorchtastic sex and healthy heapings of snark), but her shifters will stop at nothing to claim the women they love.

Georgette has worn many hats in life: newspaper reporter, EMT, internet marketer, cocktail waitress, temp, nurse's aide (not in chronological order).

When she's not rescuing fur-babies, she spends her days in a fantasy universe where she nudges her smart-mouthed, take-no-gruff heroines onto paths which will set them on a collision course with true love.

FOLLOW GEORGETTE:

Facebook
www.facebook.com/georgettewrites
Newsletter
georgettewrites.com/newsletter
Website
georgettewrites.com

MATED TO THE CAPO

Georgette St Clair

Georgette St Clair

Printed in Great Britain
by Amazon